Wylde Scott

Imagination is everything.

An imprint of Wylde Scott Entertainment, LLC
Copyright © 2015 Wylde Scott

Wylde Scott and Wylde Press are trademarks of
Wylde Scott Entertainment, LLC.

For information contact directly at
www.wyldescott.com

Library of Congress Catalog Card Number:
2015902667

ISBN: 978-0-9960315-2-3

Book Design by *the*BookDesigners, Fairfax, CA

Edited by Author Connections, LLC

For Maria
The very first believer.

SEASIDE

WYLDE SCOTT

ILLUSTRATED BY THE WONDERFUL AND TALENTED
HANNAH K SHUPING

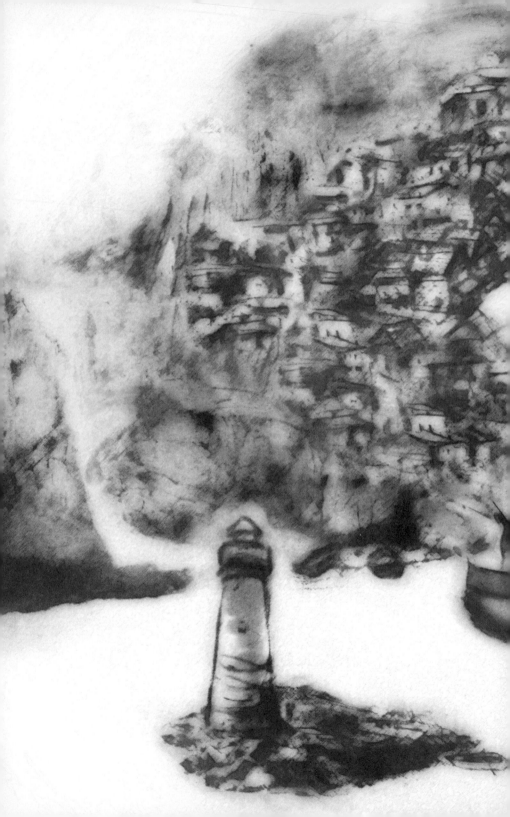

I'm not going to make it, he thought. The waves were getting higher with each stroke. Bobby's arms were tired and his mouth was now filling with more water than air. The salt was sticking to his throat, each time he drew a breath and choked on the sea. He had stopped any real swimming some time ago, and was now stuck in a desperate up and down fight. There was no turning back. He was farther from shore than Dead Bone Island.

No longer could he see the boys who had dared him to make the swim. It didn't matter anyway, he had failed their test. His body would wash up along the rocks, and they would all agree that he wasn't meant to be one of Blackbeard's Boys.

Bobby gasped as his legs gave out. There wasn't enough

energy left to scream for help. The clouds above him spun in circles and huge rain drops began to pound against the water. Alone, Bobby slipped under the waves for the final time.

Walter rushed toward the reef, his tentacles gliding quickly over the kelp beneath him. Darkness crept ahead as the sun above the water disappeared. The currents churned and kicked up the sea-bed, telling the young octopus he was in for a storm.

Through the thickening water he could see Graydon's statue guarding the reef. He was almost there when he heard her voice.

"Again?"

"Mom," answered Walter, stopping in his tracks.

"Walter Aluiscious Octopus!" began his mother, Ophelia. She was large and imposing, even in a good mood. When she was mad like this, she was a deep, deep purple, and

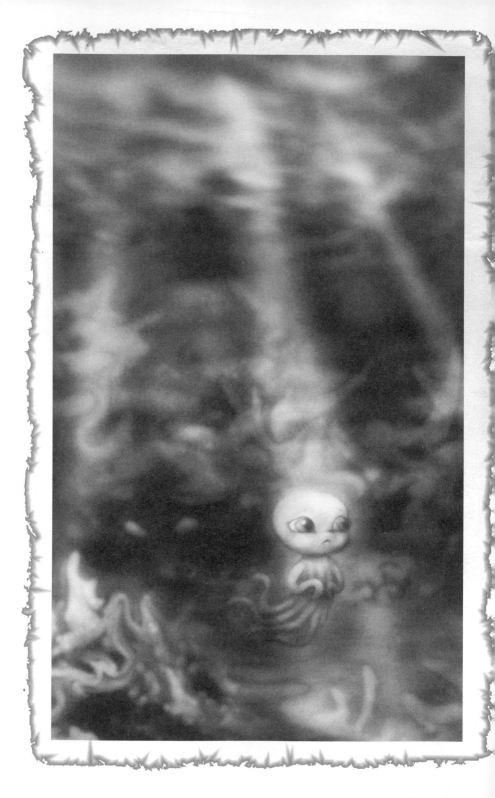

downright frightening. "How many times have you been warned?" she continued.

"But, Mom," Walter attempted.

"Do you want to end up like your grandfather?"

Walter looked up at a giant rock that had been carved into the shape of an enormous octopus.

"Like what, a hero?" he questioned in a smart tone.

"Dead." It was obvious from the way her voice cracked that this was more than a touchy subject for Walter's mother. Her father had been a hero to the reef. It was a great story everyone loved to tell, time and time again. For Ophelia, it was just the story of how she had lost her father.

"Get moving, now!" she shouted. Ophelia was done having this argument.

Walter headed home in anger. He was so mad he didn't notice how far he was swimming ahead of his mother. When she began to shout his name, he ignored her.

"Walter!" he could hear behind him.

"Walter!" she shouted again.

He kept going.

"Walter!" she screamed again.

He knew when his mother was mad at him. He had heard that tone a thousand times. This last scream was different, though. When he heard it again...

"WAALTEERRRR!!"

He stopped.

Bobby opened his eyes just enough to see the hard rain coming down on his face. He watched as a long, thin shadow stepped over him. Wet and shivering from the cold, his body ached with pain. He could hear the ocean, the waves and thunder, but had no idea where he was or how long he had been laying there.

Bobby felt himself go limp as the shadowy figure lifted his body. His mind snapped dark images, slipping in and out of consciousness. He could see black rocks, a bright light from what seemed to be the top of a tower, and a long set of stairs. His eyes shut again.

The next time he woke, Bobby was warm and wrapped in blankets, but the bed wasn't his. It was small, like a box, a spec in the

cavernous room surrounding him. The walls were made of white brick and reached up forever into a dark ceiling. Furnishings were sparse. A wooden table with a single chair, a black pot belly stove, and a rocking chair. The rest was empty space. The only light in the room flickered from a large fireplace. Above it he could see a staircase that circled the walls until they disappeared.

"You're Seamus' boy," came a voice from the frail figure standing by the fireplace. It was more statement than question.

Bobby's eyes adjusted to see an old man who looked like he had been alive for a thousand years. A full white beard covered a bronze, wrinkled face. He wore a thick brown sweater that easily weighed more than his tiny frame, a frayed captain's hat, and worn boots.

"Where am I?" asked Bobby. An uneasy feeling set in.

"The lighthouse," bristled the old man.

"The lighthouse? Dead Bone Island? You mean I made it?" asked Bobby with excitement.

"Humph. That's one way to put it," he grunted. "Lucky you're not dead."

"You must be Old Man Higgins. I mean, Mr. Higgins," said Bobby. He couldn't remember when he had seen the man in person, but this was the lighthouse, and Higgins was the lighthouse keeper. Then there was the missing arm.

Higgins reached into a pot hanging over the middle of the fire. He slopped a large ladle of thick stew into a bowl and walked it over to Bobby. It was impressive what the old man could do with his only hand.

"Eat. As soon as the storm lets up we'll get you back to the shore."

"What time is it?" asked Bobby.

Again, the old man didn't answer. He just stared into the fire as if the answers to life were unfolding in the flames. Bobby looked at the bowl in his lap. Everyone in Seaside was raised on fish stew from birth. He picked up the spoon and placed a bit in his mouth. It wasn't bad. It wasn't very good either, but Bobby was suddenly hungry. Must've been the long swim, he thought. In barely an instant, the bowl was empty.

Higgins turned at the sound of Bobby scraping the wooden spoon against the bowl. Slowly he made his way back, refilled the bowl from the pot above the fire, and handed it back to the boy.

"You remind me of your father."

"My father? You know him?" asked Bobby in surprise.

"Aye, it was he who was the last to make the challenge. Sat here the same as you, not all that long ago."

"The challenge?" This couldn't be right, thought Bobby.

"Your father was the last one to make the swim out to Dead Bone Island; about your age when he did it."

"My Father? Seamus O'Malley?" Bobby asked again.

"Aye, was a good bit smaller then," answered Higgins.

"But, my father... is afraid of the water."

"Wasn't always so," he assured the boy.

"Are you saying my father was one of Blackbeard's Boys?!?" said Bobby in complete disbelief.

"Aye, just like your grandfather before him."

A thought leapt into Bobby's mind like a fox chasing a rabbit down a hole. Higgins... the lighthouse keeper... the man with the missing arm... had been there that terrible night. He was one of the original Blackbeard's Boys. He was on the ship with Bobby's grandfather and half the men of Seaside when it crashed on the rocks. Higgins had been there, and was the only man to survive. Others talked about it, but he was there.

Bobby removed the blanket from around him and walked over to the fire where the old man was standing.

"Mr. Higgins," Bobby asked slowly, "would you tell me about that night?"

Higgins looked at the boy, surprised. He hadn't expected the question.

"Don't talk about it," Higgins answered, shaking his head.

"Please," Bobby pleaded. "My father won't speak of it. I want to know what happened. I want to know the truth - about the ship, about my grandfather, about the monster."

The old man turned away from the boy. It was there, in the reflection of the flames in his eyes; the terrible truth, the death of twenty men, the sadness of an entire village.

"Please Mr. Higgins. I need to know what really happened."

Higgins drew in a deep breath.

"It was a night very much like this," he started. "The ship was already filled with fish. We had been on the grandest expedition. But the captain, Rodrigo Bonicelli, he was no ordinary captain, always had to push for more. One more net filled with fish, one more great whale to bring home. Your grandfather was his first mate. I was his second. As we headed home we towed the large net, just to see what we might catch. Sure enough, we caught it... the catch to end all catches."

"Was it as large as they say?" asked Bobby, his eyes opened wide.

Higgins continued the story in a trance-like state, his eyes journeying further into the fire. "The ship came upon its side so quickly, the sails dipping in the water, the masts falling like trees. As the line tore through the deck, the stern sung its way around and the first few men went overboard. They were the lucky ones. By the time those left stood up and found our bearings, it was too late. The ship was hung up, and we were sitting prey. I was standing at the side of the ship when it came. A beast so extraordinary, none of us had ever seen anything like it. It rose twenty feet above the ship. Its arms were everywhere. The captain, ever the fisherman, was the first to react. As the beast began to tear the ship apart, the captain took to the harpoon. Ten, fifteen times he shot, again and again, and yet, nothing. Nothing would stop the monster. With my own eyes I watched it wrap the captain in its tentacles and squeeze him like a doll. Your grandfather, he was as brave a man as any. He jumped after the captain, and together they went overboard. A rope from one of the harpoons caught my arm. Before I knew it I was in the water. I watched that powerful creature crush the ship along the reef, like a child stomping toys. The men were all gone."

"How did you survive?" asked Bobby.

Higgins grabbed the shoulder where his arm used to be. "I was lucky. The beast dove for the depths of the sea, and carried me with him on the ropes. I lost breath, and awoke on the rocks... the arm was gone."

"And my grandfather?"

Higgins was lost. The fire in front of him was now all consuming, the flames dredging up painful memories. When his eyes returned to the room, he was done talking.

"Eat. The storm will let up soon."

W alter fought with all of his might to hold on to his mother's tentacle.

"Go, Walter! Swim!" Ophelia shouted at her son. "Swim away!"

Walter wouldn't listen. He knew something terrible was happening. The sea floor had lost its tranquil beauty. It was black and violent. He could barely see her through the spinning sand. The fish often talked about watching loved ones vanish into the sky above. His mother had warned him so many times. The stories were always horrifying. And now, it was right in front of him.

In the storm above a fearsome whaling ship called the *Black Fin* was tossing and turning in the raging swells, its net dragging Ophelia across the ocean floor.

"Pull!" bellowed Antonio Bonicelli, the ship's captain. The giant fisherman with wild dark eyes and heavy black beard was standing straight up in the blistering storm surrounding him. "Pull!"

The seas were angry, and the skies worse. Lightning cracked along the bottom of the clouds and thunder fought with the howling wind to see who could sound more ominous.

"Pull!" cried Bonicelli again.

Water crashed over the deck as the crew fought to keep the ship afloat. Giant waves kept it rolling from side to side. Barrels and crates sped up and down the deck as sailors washed overboard, disappearing forever into the midnight sea below. The lucky few still on board were frightened. They wanted to go home, but Bonicelli would hear none of that. He was from a long line of brave fishermen who had faced the worst of the sea. He puffed his rolling chest high in the air and wrapped his beast-like arms around the heaviest rope. His weathered and scarred face turned straight into the storm's harshest winds.

This was no time to go back. He was finally here, the end of a life-long dream. It had begun with his great-grandfather and continued through several generations. He had lost his father to the same obsession many years before. Tonight, he would finally be victorious.

"Pull!" shouted Bonicelli, his eyes spinning with madness. "PULL!"

"Swim!" Ophelia screamed, fighting the nets with every ounce of strength.

Walter wouldn't let go. Ophelia pushed her tentacles through the holes in the net and dug them into the sand. Long lines scraped across the sea-bed swirling around her. Walter noticed something deep in his mother's eyes that he had never seen before. She was scared.

Before he could react, she pulled one of her tentacles out of the sand, then reached over and grabbed his.

"Walter, go now!"

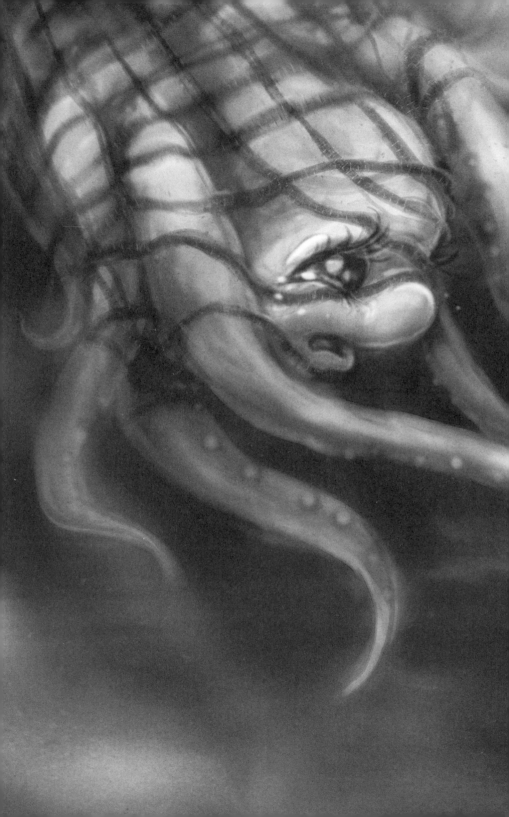

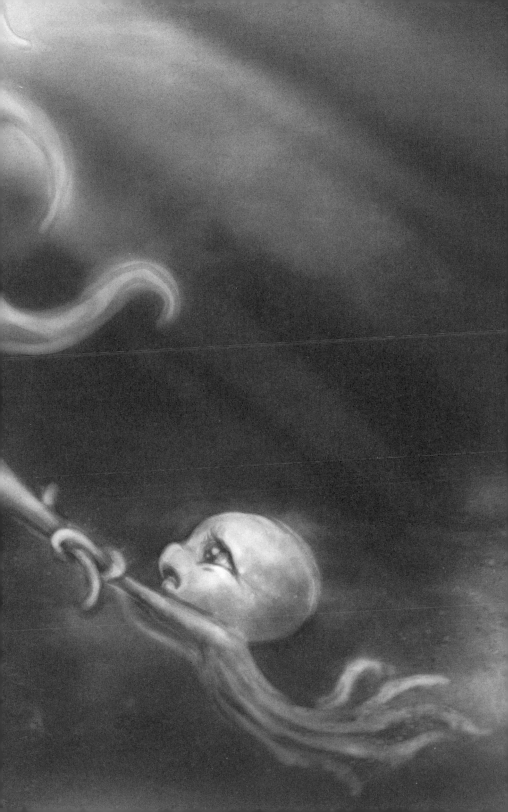

As she released his small tentacles from hers, the net swept Ophelia away with incredible speed. She disappeared into the blackness above.

"Do we have her?" Bonicelli asked as he rushed to the side of his ship. There... just over the side, hanging in the net. Right there in front of him... there she was.

"I've done it!" he shouted at the top of his lungs, fists pumping into the air. Lightning ripped through the sky as rain poured down on his face.

"I am the greatest fisherman of all time!"

Higgins rapped on the door of the small house with his good arm. Bobby's eyes were glued to the floor. The rain had stopped, but the cobblestones below his feet were still wet. The door swept open quickly. Too afraid to look up, Bobby recognized his father's boots.

"Bobby! Where have you been? We were looking everywhere for you. You had me frightened son," blasted his father, stooping down to hug his son even though he was obviously upset.

"Seamus," nodded Higgins.

"Higgins? What... how did you find him?" asked Seamus.

"Lad made the swim. I brought him home," answered Higgins.

"Swim? What swim?" asked Seamus, not fully understanding.

"The challenge. Dead Bone Island," added Higgins.

Bobby knew what was coming.

"Dead Bone Island?"

He saw his father's eyes light up with fury as it began to sink in. His father drew in a deep breath as if he were preparing to blow down the walls of the house.

"Dead Bone Island!" he repeated at twice the volume, not knowing where to begin. Before he could start, Bobby fired a thought he hoped might grant him a reprieve from the trouble he was in.

"You did it!"

"What?" his father stopped.

"You did it. You made the swim to Dead Bone Island. You were one of Blackbeard's Boys!" Bobby blurted with a certain satisfaction.

Mr. O'Malley was caught off guard. It was something he had never told Bobby, and it was a shock to hear it now. He looked over at Higgins in surprise.

"Well, glad the boy's safe. Need to get back to the lighthouse. Good evening," Higgins stated as he hurried to leave.

"Good evening," answered Mr. O'Malley.

"Goodnight," mumbled Bobby under his breath.

Mr. O'Malley closed the door and thought for a moment before saying anything. Bobby knew his dad was trying to think of a way to express himself without yelling. It wasn't meant to be any less stern.

"Bobby," Seamus started, looking his son straight in the eyes, "what have I told you about listening to those boys?"

"But you were one of them. Why can't I be one of Blackbeard's Boys if you were, and Grandpa was? I don't understand," answered Bobby.

Every boy in Seaside for more than three generations had wanted to be one. From the time they could hold their very first fishing pole it was all they thought about. Every captain on every ship had been one. It was the top of the food chain. Membership meant a certain status among the town, a guaranteed path to a celebrated position, and likely your own ship one day. The not so secret club made up the pecking order of who would be first in line to go to sea. If you couldn't get in you would likely end up swabbing decks, or maybe pulling nets, or worse, stuck on shore.

"You can't just do things because someone else chooses to," Mr. O'Malley responded, avoiding the bigger question.

"Not just someone. Everyone," Bobby interrupted.

"Everyone wants to be one of Blackbeard's Boys. I want to be one, just like you were, and I made the swim, just like you did!"

"Do you have any idea what could have happened to you?" his father demanded. "What if you hadn't made it? What if you would have drowned or been washed out to sea? What if..."

"What if the monster would have gotten me like it got Grandpa?"

Mr. O'Malley went silent. That was the point, wasn't it. Bobby was never going to see what it was he feared so much. And while it was simple for a ten year old to dismiss, there were dangers in the world that Bobby's young and adventurous mind wasn't ready to accept. Seamus O'Malley wasn't ever going to forget it.

"Go to your room, Bobby. We'll talk about this in the morning."

"But," tried Bobby.

"Your room," finished Mr. O'Malley, leaving no doubt that the conversation had ended.

As Bobby stomped his feet up the stairs in protest, one thought repeated over and over in his head, "My father, one of Blackbeard's Boys!" *How could he not have known this?*

"Blackbeard's Boys..." his mouth spoke out loud.

This changed everything.

33

Walter had spent the entire night at the foot of his grandfather's statue. Staring up at the enormous figure, he wondered if his grandfather had actually been that large. The tentacles were at least five times the length of Walter's, and as thick as a dolphin's body. The head rose another ten feet, nearly reaching the surface of the water. Shimmering rays cast from the sun above bounced around it, making it appear even larger than the truth that had inspired it.

Graydon was the only one who had ever been brave enough to fight the two-leggers. He had saved many lives that day. No one was even sure why he had done it. When the net hung up on the reef, Graydon fought back, destroying the ship and setting everyone free.

But even the great octopus had not survived the battle. He was a hero, yes, but a dead one. There were no other stories of anyone coming back from the nets. Walter knew exactly what that meant.

"Grandpa, what should I do?" he asked.

Walter knew the answer, even if his grandfather wasn't there to tell him. Deep inside he had none of the bravery Graydon had shown. Walter was afraid. Even so, he summoned what little courage was inside of him, and turned away from the reef. As he swam toward the place where the two-leggers lived, his head filled with his mother's warnings.

From the water, Seaside had a daunting appearance. The lighthouse on Dead Bone Island stood out as a beacon of treacherous ground. The island itself guarded the town's only inlet. Its black stones were covered in the bones of fish and deadwood from old shipwrecks. Beyond it, two jagged cliffs dove sharply into the sea, marking the mouth of the harbor. Sailors had only yards to navigate through the narrow passes on either side. The distance to the island wasn't all that close, but there were shallow dangers everywhere.

Walter never went into the harbor. As he reached the mouth, he perched himself low in the water along the jagged shoreline of the cliffs. From his usual spot he could see the odd little village nestled among the rocks. He had seen all of his previous visits as adventures, filled with wonder and surprise. From a distance everything had seemed comfortable and safe. The houses glowed with warm color and life, the ships sailing in and out were majestic, and the two-legged creatures busily walking around - fascinating.

Now he felt a belly full of guppies. No longer could he watch from a safe distance. If he was going to find his mother, Walter would have to enter the harbor. He would have to approach the huge ships, and maybe even fight one of the two-legged creatures he had so long admired. Fear began to overwhelm him. Tears filled his eyes.

"Would you pleeeeeeease stop all that crying!" cried a voice echoing from the rocks. "You are ruining my nap!"

Startled, Walter sunk into the water and looked around.

"Hellloooo!" cried the voice again, "I can see you. You're not fooling anybody with the hiding."

Walter's eyes shot up and spotted the origin of the voice. Perched high above him sat an extremely short and rotund pelican, barely noticeable among the white, black and grey of the cliffs.

"What's the matter? No speak-a-de-English? I am trying to sleep. So please take your sniveling and sobbing and go-somewhere else!" shouted the pelican.

"But..." started Walter.

"Uh, uh, uh, no ifs, ands or buts. I am going back to my nap, and you are going to take your blubbering somewhere else," the pelican urged as he turned slightly around on his perch and closed his eyes. "I'm laying down now. I'm closing my eyes. When I awake, you will be gone."

Walter didn't move.

The pelican opened one eye, slowly. "Oy jeeeze, this is going to be a long day. Look you... what are you, anyway?" asked the Pelican.

Walter rose up just a bit more from the water. "Me?"

"Yes, you! The little blue thing hiding in the water!"

"I... I'm an octopus," answered Walter.

The pelican began to laugh hysterically. "An octopus!" he replied. "Oh that's funny. Octopuses are big and scary with twenty arms, and live at the bottom of the sea. They have giant mouths with a hundred teeth. Everyone knows that."

Walter wasn't very big, and he had never seen himself as scary, but he was most definitely an octopus. Of that he was certain.

"Octopuses only have eight tentacles," he replied, as he raised his own eight arms out of the water.

The pelican took another look at Walter and screamed as he attempted to take off. In the panic he forgot about the wall behind him and smacked right into it. His round body bounced off several rocks on the way down, before landing in the water.

He screamed again as he backed into the rocks behind him. "Please, don't eat me!"

"I'm not going to eat you. You're funny," Walter chuckled, and for a second he forgot the sadness in his heart.

"Then why are you bothering me?" asked the pelican.

"I didn't mean to," answered Walter. "I'm looking for my mother. Her name is Ophelia."

"Well, no octopuses around here; except you, of course. So

I guess you'll be looking somewhere else."

The pelican slowly backed his way out of the water and onto the shore, where he shook off his feathers, all the while keeping his eyes carefully fixated on Walter.

"Nice meeting ya kid. See you around."

"Wait!" begged Walter. "I know where she is."

"Well then, what are you asking me for?"

"She was captured in one of those nets on the big ships, where the two-leggers take all the fish."

"You mean the fishing boats? Sounds like a tough break, kid. I wish you all the luck in the world in finding her."

"Can't you help me?" asked Walter.

"What?" replied the pelican.

"Will you help me?" asked Walter again.

"Help you what?"

"Have you ever been to where the boats are? Where the two-leggers live?"

"What? Seaside? Sure kid, that's my town. They love me there. Now that you mention it, it's getting pretty close to my lunch time."

"Can you take me there?" Walter asked.

"Well, I don't know. I'm pretty busy with lunch and all," the pelican said.

"I just need to find the boat, that's all. Just help me find the one she's on, and I won't ask for anything else," pleaded Walter.

"What's in it for me?" asked the pelican.

"How about I don't eat you." Walter mustered the most ominous grumble that he could as he rose up on his tentacles until he stood above the pelican. He held the pose for as long as he could before cracking a smile. Walter wasn't very good at being scary. They both began to laugh.

The pelican said, "I like your sense of humor, kid. What's your name?"

"I'm Walter."

"Name's Pucello. If there's anyone who can find your mom, you're looking at him."

The boys' faces were white when Bobby entered the schoolhouse. No one said a word as he walked in and sat down in his chair in the third row. As the class worked through the morning routine, first spelling, then math, whispers floated around the room. It wasn't until they made it outside for recess in the back of the schoolhouse that Mario approached Bobby.

Mario was two years older and almost a good foot taller than Bobby. He stood directly in Bobby's face, to intimidate him. This had resulted in a scuffle between the two boys more than once, and Mr. O'Malley had punished Bobby the last time it happened.

"We thought you were dead, Gracie," started the older boy.

Robert Grace O'Malley. That was Bobby's full name. He never understood why his mother had chosen to give him a girl's

middle name. It gave Mario great pleasure to taunt him with it.

"Fish food," added Pete, a freckle-faced kid and Mario's sidekick. A semi-circle gathered around to witness the confrontation. This was the current lot of kids that made up Blackbeard's Boys.

"Leave him alone, Mario!" shouted a small voice.

Rachel, an eight-year old girl with long, dark brown curls and a round, porcelain face broke through the ranks. She was Mario's little sister, and all too familiar with his mean ways. When she was four he had taken her favorite doll and fed it to the butcher's dog. When she was six he had ruined an entire picnic she'd spent hours laying out for her friends, because he wanted her blanket for a tent he was building. Even as recently as this summer, he had placed a beetle bug on a spoon and covered it in ice cream before feeding it to her. There was no end to his cruelty.

Bobby hated Rachel defending him. He didn't need defending. Especially not by an eight year-old girl. He could defend himself.

"Go back to your dolls," Mario shouted as he pushed her out of the circle with his hand on her face. The boys closed their flanks tightly so she could not get back in.

"I made it! I made it to Dead Bone Island," Bobby responded

with pride. "That's more than I can say for all of you," he added defiantly.

"Are you calling me a liar, O'Malley?" threatened Mario.

"Higgins told me. The last one to make it out there alone was my father, Seamus O'Malley."

The boys all began to laugh.

"That's a funny one, Gracie. Everyone knows your father is afraid of the water. Shows you what a kook that old lighthouse keeper, Higgins, is. Maybe no one saw us because none of us needed to be rescued."

"I made it. I deserve to join the crew!" demanded Bobby.

"I'm the captain, and I say who gets to be one of us, and who doesn't," replied Mario. "You know the rules, O'Malley. I said three challenges. Dead Bone Island was only the first. You still have to complete two more."

"Fine. I'm not afraid. What's the next challenge?"

A grin crept across Mario's face. He had been dreaming up this one for a long time and had saved it just for Bobby.

"Bonicelli's ship," he said with a sinister tone, "you have to sneak onto Bonicelli's ship and steal something that only he would have."

CHAPTER SEVEN

"What?" asked Bobby. "No one else ever had to do that!"

"I thought you weren't afraid, Gracie."

"But..."

Before Bobby could protest, the gathering was interrupted.

"What is going on here?" Ms. Peach, the town's school-teacher, yelled from outside the circle. "Mario Martinello, are you fighting? Robert? What is going on here?" Rachel was standing behind her with a smile.

"Nothing, Ms. Peach," answered all of the boys as they dispersed quickly.

Ms. Peach looked at Bobby, searching for the truth. Behind her, Mario drew a finger across his throat, to warn Bobby what would happen if he spoke. Bobby knew better. No one respected a tattletale. He had made it through the first challenge. He certainly wasn't going to ruin his chances now.

easide had been a fishing village for more than one hundred years. It was an odd place to find a town of any sort, and Seaside was odd in just about every way. The rise up from the harbor was steep and formidable. The houses were bent and leaned in every direction. The streets were crooked and winding. No two cobblestones were the same length or height. The only flat space in the entire town was the market square. It was as though a painter had spilled a bucket filled with brushes, and everything in the town had been painted among the rocky cliffs. Behind it rose a set of white-capped mountains. Only one perilous road existed between the town and the valleys beyond.

From the shops surrounding the square, tiny wood-framed houses with brightly colored walls and shingled rooftops moved up and away from the shoreline. On the north side up a small slope stood the town church, the largest building in Seaside, which doubled as the children's schoolhouse.

As Pucello made his way through the village, Walter followed along the shoreline; staying low in the water to remain undetected.

Mr. Rupenstoop, a funny man with a long, crane-like neck, who wore an unusually tall hat and long coat, recognized Pucello and called out to the bird.

"Why Pucello, is it lunch time already?"

Pucello continued down Market Street, a narrow cobblestone path that led away from the square and over a small walking bridge. The street ended at the fish market, which spanned the top of the town's aging docks. This was Pucello's favorite place.

It was always busy. The smell of fish filled the salty air. Seagulls dove from above to catch any scraps being thrown away.

Pucello launched himself toward the top of a barrel, but didn't quite make the jump. A jolly fisherman named Dursten laughed hysterically as Pucello flopped backwards, his webbed feet straight up in the air. Pucello struggled to roll over. He tried once more, falling on his face this time. Dursten laughed again, his belly jiggling like a water balloon.

"You silly bird," Dursten muttered as he rolled off the last few giggles, "always good for a laugh."

Walter watched from among the rocks and piers, struggling to maintain sight of the fat pelican as it waddled its way among the two-leggers. At every turn he was afraid of being caught.

The large ships the fisherman took to sea could be found lined up along the docks. Men moved up and down long rows of pilings and planks while large nets hoisted the day's haul to the fish market just above the landing.

The ships were massive and powerful, built for rough seas and heavy nets. The largest were the cargo ships, made to carry large loads over great distances in as little time as possible. Smaller but just as mighty were the whaling ships, built for long voyages and pure hunting. All had long bows that curved and pointed toward the sun, and thick hulls made of strong woods, with portholes lined ten, sometimes fifteen in a row. Some ship decks could hold as many as thirty men working at the same time. The masts stood straight and strong, three in a row, towering up to the clouds. It was a sight to behold.

Pucello flopped his way down the long set of stairs, two and three at a time or as far as a short flap of his wings would take him, until he reached the lower docks where the men boarded the ships. The whole flying thing was just too much work. It always made the fishermen laugh. Besides, he never flew when he was this hungry. He began to wonder how long this whole adventure was going to take.

"Well, which one?" he whispered down to Walter in the water below him.

"I'm not sure," Walter replied, "they all look so similar from down here."

Together they moved up and down the docks, checking what ships they could. One by one, Pucello climbed barrels and crates, looked up onto decks and peeped into portholes. No sign of an octopus anywhere.

Finally they came upon a very dark ship. It was a whale hunter, but different from the others. The damp woods were almost black, tired, and worn from years at sea. The sails, once white, were now colored in a deep brown. The ropes were old, thick and green. Its great hull was chipped and beaten, the huge wheel at the helm missing teeth. This ship had certainly seen its

days, and those days looked terrifying. Walter shuddered just looking at it. He felt as though the water grew colder and the clouds gathered above him. He didn't want to go any closer. But somehow he knew - this was the one.

The village was full of great fishermen, but the whalers were the bravest of the sea. They could claim the largest catches and the fiercest battles. No one was mightier than Antonio Bonicelli. Town taverns were filled with colorful tales of this great fisherman; how, on one journey, when all of his crew had jumped out of a small boat in fear, he single-handedly held on to a rope tied to a massive black whale. He battled the giant for what seemed like an eternity, until the small boat disappeared from sight. Late at night they found him, miles and miles away, smiling. The whale, which had grown tired first and lost the battle, floated lifelessly next to him.

On another expedition, Antonio had hauled in a great white shark, only to be bitten as he tried to remove the shark from his net. With one arm caught deep in the shark's teeth, he jumped onto the shark's back and peeled its jaws open, then punched the shark to sleep, in anger.

The tales were many, but Bonicelli himself had long ago lost interest in them. Even with all of the stories, Bonicelli had never quite received the respect or adulation from the town that his ancestors had. He felt slighted by their simple recognition of his profession rather than true admiration of his greatness. Sure, he had caught hundreds of whales, but so had his father. No one alive in Seaside today could claim a larger shark catch, but his great grandfather could.

In fact, there was only one beast of the sea that no one could lay claim to. Not anyone in Seaside. Not anyone in his family. His father had been drug to the bottom of the sea trying to get one. No one had even tried since, except for Bonicelli. And at this moment, he had outdone them all.

"Oh, how I've dreamed of this day!" he whispered to himself in disbelief.

Bonicelli was practically giddy as he pranced around his captain's quarters alone. With a bottle in one hand he walked along a row of family pictures hanging on the wall

and toasted them one by one; ten generations of fishermen going back nearly two hundred years.

"Great-great grandpapa... Great grandpapa... Grandpapa... Papa..." For a moment Antonio stopped and stared at his father's picture. He had been only a boy when he last saw him. Rodrigo Bonicelli was a harsh captain and an unforgiving father. Antonio couldn't remember a single praise or compliment his father had ever offered him. It was almost enough to draw a tear from his eye now, but then he remembered what he was celebrating.

"Oh, Papa, you would be so proud! Tomorrow we will show this town!"

Out of pure joy, a song rose from inside him...

"Oh how I've dreamed of this day
When everyone will finally say
There he goes, the greatest fisherman of all!

Sharks, they've nothing but teeth
A dozen I've caught in my sleep
They run and hide every time I set sail for the sea!

Whales I'll leave to Ahab,

That hunt is so boring and drab,

They're so slow, it's really no challenge for me.

Some fish by the pound...

Casting their nets all around...

But not me, I'll hunt the worst of the sea!

Oh what a day it will be...

Now everyone will be talking about me...

Bonicelli, the greatest fisherman of all!"

Just outside the cabin, a set of eyes watched the jubilant fisherman through round portholes.

"This has got to be the ship," whispered Pucello as he jumped off a crate.

"What? Why? Is she there? Did you see her?

"SHHHH!" Pucello scolded as he moved along the piled crates to find another porthole.

Walter couldn't stand it anymore. To his right a long, black, algae-stained rope descended from the deck to the piling below.

Walter wrapped his tentacles around the piling beneath the dock and shimmied his way up until he could reach the rope. Grabbing onto it, he swung his tentacles one over the other and made his way across the span of water until he reached a porthole of his own. There, at precisely the same time, from opposite sides of the ship, Walter and Pucello spotted her.

In the cargo hold below were Mr. Frimp and Mr. Frump, Bonicelli's first and second mates. On the cruel side, much like their captain, they were having fun taunting their capture. Both holding long wooden sticks, they danced around a large cage, banging the bars and jumping in and out, staying just far enough away to avoid her grip.

In the middle of the cage stood a defiant Ophelia. Out of the water she was a huge and terrifying creature, but then again, she was a prisoner being held against her will, and not happy to be there. Her angry eyes watched as her jailers danced around her. When she had had enough, she struck back.

Frimp raised his stick over his head when a long thick tentacle flew through the bars of the cage, wrapping around his body and snapping him up. He began to scream as Ophelia shook him in the air.

Frump's jaw dropped to the floor at the site of his mate in the octopus' grasp. For a moment he stood frightened, then rushed toward the cage and began to pound his stick on Ophelia's tentacle.

With great force another tentacle rushed through the bars in the cage and snapped the stick from Frump's hand. A third tentacle swooped in behind him and swiped him up off of his feet. Ophelia hung him upside down and shook him with even greater force. She was furious. Frimp and Frump joined each other in a chorus of terrified screams.

A loud SNAP interrupted the excitement. It was Bonicelli, standing in the open doorway holding a long cat-o-nine tails, his favorite punishing device. He raised his giant arm and swung the grip in his hand as hard as he could toward the floor. The tails of the whip rolled through the air, cracking again, the ends snapping on the tentacle holding up Frimp.

Ophelia felt the sting run through her entire body. She

dropped Frimp and Frump and coiled up in the corner of the cage. Bonicelli walked closer to remind her who was in charge. The great fisherman and the massive octopus stared into each other's eyes.

The sun was setting as Walter and Pucello sat on the rocks along the shoreline. Walter's eyes were glued to the ship where his mother was being held, the tears returning to his eyes.

"We have to get her," Walter said, not sure how, only that he had to find a way.

"We can't," said Pucello, "it's too dangerous."

"What if the ship leaves? What if they hurt her? Or worse?"

Pucello looked into Walter's eyes as he struggled for a good answer. What had started as an afternoon escapade had turned into more than he had bargained for. All he'd wanted a few hours ago was to fill his belly with fish and return to his nap. Now it was too late. He liked the young octopus, and he knew what would become of the mother if they left her there. Walter certainly wasn't going to give up on saving Ophelia. If Pucello didn't help him, things were certain to end badly.

"We have to come up with a plan," he said, thinking out loud.

They couldn't walk onto the ship and simply ask for her. Bonicelli and his men weren't going to let her go. How could they slip onto the ship undetected, and get her out of the cage without being caught themselves?

"There's only one way," muttered Pucello. "We'll have to go back when they're all asleep. We'll go back tonight."

It was rare that Bonicelli changed out of his fishing clothes, but this was a special occasion, and Ms. Peach was a special lady. It had been a while since he had last visited her. Gone was the heavy wool cap that normally adorned his head. His hair was carefully combed back and held in place with an oily tonic. The thick sweater he usually wore to beat out the cold was replaced with a shirt and a dress jacket his mother had once given to his father. His large, heavy fishing boots had been taken off, and in their place he wore a pair of brown dress up, laced boots. Truth be told, he looked quite decent.

As he splashed cologne over his thick beard and rubbed it down his neck, he smiled into the mirror. "Hello you handsome devil," he purred before heading out.

The evening had started as it normally did in the O'Malley home. First, Bobby and his father had dinner together. It usually consisted of light conversation with a laugh or two about something that transpired in school or in town. Tonight, however, the table was silent. Mr. O'Malley and Bobby both ate their entire meal without a single word to each other. They had barely spoken since Bobby's return from Dead Bone Island. He was sure at any moment he was going to hear the extended punishment his father had laid out for him. Yet nothing came.

Seamus O'Malley was a tall, thin man with a warm smile and kind eyes. Dinner was normally followed by a playful wrestling match on the living room floor. Matches consisted of tickling each other until Bobby cried STOP, with tears running down his face from laughing so hard. This would typically end with someone getting hurt; nothing serious, just a bump on the table or a scratched elbow by accident. Now that it was just the two of them there was no one to stop the rough-housing. Bobby loved these times together, but tonight there would be no match.

"Straight to the bath, and then bed," his father finally spoke.

Mr. O'Malley supervised Bobby's bedtime routine quietly from the door. Bobby pulled his arm through the second pajama sleeve and pulled his head through the hole at the top.

"Say your prayers and hop in the sack," his father commanded softly.

Bobby kneeled next to the bed. It was a short prayer.

"God bless our home, my dad, and mommy in heaven. Amen."

He climbed quickly into bed and pulled the covers up to his chest. Mr. O'Malley turned out the light and softly shut the door behind him. It was unusual for his father to be so curt. It unnerved Bobby.

"Goodnight, Dad," Bobby shouted, trying to get some reaction from his father.

"Goodnight, son," Mr. O'Malley responded, cracking the door open.

"Dad?" Bobby shot out as Mr. O'Malley went to leave again.

"Yes, son?"

"I miss Mommy."

"Me too, son, goodnight."

Bobby watched as the light from the hallway shrunk across

the ceiling and disappeared, then listened to his father's foot-steps. The floor boards sunk under Mr. O'Malley's feet as he made his way down the hall. Bobby could hear the stairs creak one by one as his father descended to the living room. Every night Mr. O'Malley would settle into his favorite chair and read until he fell asleep, his round glasses sliding from his nose. Bobby heard his father's chair as the legs scratched the floor, then waited for the familiar sound of the book falling from his father's grip. It usually didn't take very long, but he couldn't risk making noise while his father was still awake. Thankfully, Mr. O'Malley was a sound sleeper. Bobby knew he wouldn't see his father awake again before breakfast. Before long he heard the quiet but familiar thump of the book hitting the floor.

His eyes turned to the open window and the clock tower in the town square. The night was clear and the stars were shin-ing. From where the house stood you couldn't see the docks, but Bobby could picture them just beyond the tower. The half-moon was nearly over the clock. He would have to hurry.

Bobby lifted his head to hear if any sounds were coming from the first floor. Nothing. His heart pounded as he pushed the covers slowly off of his legs. With every move, his heartbeat grew louder. As his feet gently touched the floor, it took him almost a minute to stand on his full weight. His mouth began to run dry and sweat filled his palms. Upon standing, he froze for several seconds without a single breath. Convinced he had successfully gotten out of bed without waking his father downstairs, he moved to the window. The clock tower struck and startled him. He froze again, and waited... seven, eight, nine strikes. He stood listening another few moments, just to be sure. Then, with only the breathing of the house and the crickets outside, he pushed forward.

It wasn't the first time he had climbed down the tree outside his window, but tonight for some reason it seemed a whole lot higher. The branches seemed further from the window than he remembered. He could try to walk down the stairs and out the door through the kitchen, but those stairs were sure to creak. What would he tell his father if Seamus woke to find Bobby standing at the base of the stairs, fully dressed with a knapsack on his back in the middle of the night? There sure weren't any good answers he could think of. It was better to risk the tree.

From the tree Bobby could see straight into the house downstairs where his father's chair sat. The back of the chair

faced the window, and Bobby could see his father's arm hanging off the side. There, below his hand was the book, pages down, split open on the floor where it had landed. Mr. O'Malley was asleep, but somehow that didn't make Bobby feel any better. He headed off into the night, alone.

Ms. Peach, the town's schoolteacher, was baking a pie when the doorbell surprised her. It was a bit late for visitors, and it was rare that someone came to her house when she wasn't expecting company. Who could it be, she thought?

She pulled the pie out of the oven, placed it on the kitchen table and pulled off her mittens. Passing the mirror in the hall, she stopped and noticed her appearance. "Oh my," she said aloud at the sight. She quickly took off the apron full of stains and wiped the flour from her left cheek. Her hair was matted and damp with sweat from the heat of the kitchen, so she took a hairpin from a drawer and did her best to fashion a bun. Long, with deep auburn locks, her hair made a stunning contrast to her light porcelain skin. No longer a young girl, Ms. Peach was still quite a beautiful woman.

"Good evening, Ms. Peach," Bonicelli bellowed as she opened the door. He looked nervous but held a giant smile.

"Anthony, what a surprise," Ms. Peach replied curiously.

"I'm sorry, I know it's late and all, but, the men and I just returned from a grand expedition, and well, I had something I wanted to tell you and couldn't wait."

Bonicelli pulled some flowers from behind his back and shook off the dirt. It was obvious to Ms. Peach they had come from someone's garden.

"These are for you."

"Thank you. Would you like to come in?" asked Ms. Peach.

"Well, of course, if you want me to," answered Bonicelli, moving through the doorway like a cat.

"Please," answered Ms. Peach, not exactly excited about having a guest at this time of night. As she closed the door behind him, Ms. Peach looked left and right down the street. It might not look proper to the other townspeople, but she didn't want to be rude to her visitor.

"Is that pie I smell?" asked Bonicelli, taking in a deep breath that filled his lungs.

"Yes, blueberry. I just finished baking it."

"Oh, you know how I love your pies. Would it be too much to ask?"

"Of course not, Anthony," said Ms. Peach as she pointed him toward the kitchen.

Bonicelli knew exactly where the kitchen was. He had been there many times before. They had known each other for some time. As a young bride, Ms. Peach had come to Seaside with her husband in search of work. She had taken a job as the town's schoolteacher and he had gone to work on the boats, as did most men in Seaside.

Though she thought about him often, few things brought back the sad memory of her husband as much as a visit from Bonicelli. These visits always made her uncomfortable, especially when he came knocking late at night after a trip at sea. He must feel guilty, she told herself as she set a place at the table for him, but deep inside she knew it was something else.

After being at sea for so many years with his men, Bonicelli's manners were sorely lacking. Ms. Peach went to get a knife to cut the pie, and turned to see him eating directly from the tin.

She placed the knife back in the drawer and waited patiently as he gobbled it down.

Her thoughts turned to her late husband. Mr. Peach had decided to join Bonicelli's crew with a promise for better pay. As he sailed off for that trip a knot had taken hold of her stomach in a way she had never felt before. The seas were rough, but it wasn't the worst of nights, and he was quickly becoming an experienced fisherman. Sadly, he was lost at sea forever. Now all she had left was his memory, and these visits from Bonicelli.

Crumbs were clinging to all parts of his beard when he finished the pie and let out a belch. The combed hair and dress shirt couldn't completely hide what a rough cad Bonicelli actually was, despite the attempt to put on his best behavior when he was around Ms. Peach.

"That was delicious!" he proclaimed.

"I'll have to bake another one for the children," she replied.

"You must! They would love that." Bonicelli responded.

"Now if you don't mind, Anthony, I really am tired. I don't mean to be rude, but it's quite late and I must be getting to bed."

Bonicelli showed his disappointment as Ms. Peach helped him up from the chair and gently guided him toward the front door.

"But... but... I haven't told you what I came here for," he stuttered as she turned the knob.

"I'm sorry, what was it you wanted to say?" she asked politely.

"Well, I really can't tell you," he replied excitedly. "It's a surprise!"

Ms. Peach sighed.

"You must promise me that you'll come to the festival at the market square tomorrow. No later than ten o'clock," he continued. "You must promise me! This will be like nothing you've ever seen. I swear with a cross of my heart."

She was sure with Bonicelli that it probably was something rare and strange he was up to. She had every intention of being at the festival.

"Very well, Anthony, I shall see you at the square tomorrow."

"Yippee!" he yelled. The two of them stood for a moment, awkwardly staring at each other in silence.

"Goodnight, Anthony." Ms. Peach finally said.

"Goodnight, Ms. Peach," Bonicelli whispered with a grin of expectation on his face.

As he leaned in with his eyes closed and offered his cheek, Ms. Peach shut the door.

Seaside seemed like a different town in the dark. The streets were empty, hollow and cold. Missing were the smiling faces and busy town noises that Bobby was used to. No children playing outside. No mothers pounding out their rugs or sweeping the walks. No carts rattling down the cobblestone streets. In the darkness, somehow every noise seemed ten times as loud, and far more frightening.

Bobby could hear the wind moaning through the trees like a lost ghost searching for his grave. An unlatched gate swung open and then shut, sending him jumping with the bang of its handle. A spooked cat knocked over a pot as it shot from beneath his feet. But even the thick knot in Bobby's throat wouldn't keep him from joining Blackbeard's Boys. He had to succeed, in spite of the fear he was feeling. Determined to be brave, he sucked in a deep breath and kept walking.

When he reached the docks, Bobby hid nervously behind a set of barrels next to the fish market. He hadn't seen anyone except a sailor or two as they passed by. The docks were eerily

silent with the exception of the waves breaking against the pilings. He made his way down the long stairs and past the rows of
old ships.

Bobby's nerves were firing at full speed as his feet settled
on the deck of the *Black Fin*. He could hear his heart beating
in his eardrums as his eyes searched around him. Everything
seemed bigger than he had imagined. The ropes were thick and
smelled of the sea. The masts were like giant trees, reaching for
the stars in the sky. He had waited forever to see this up close,
but his excitement would have to wait. He was on a mission, and
the deck held nothing that would convince the boys he had been
on Bonicelli's ship. He moved slowly toward the back of the ship,
the deck boards underneath him groaning with each step, afraid
he would be discovered at any moment.

The ship's bridge and afterdeck stood just behind the mast
closest to the stern. On either side of the bridge stood two lad-
ders; one leading up to the ship's enormous helm, the other
leading down into the dark of the ship's hull. There was sure
to be more of Bonicelli's things below, but Bobby was afraid of
what else might be waiting for him.

Pucello hadn't noticed the small boy tiptoe past him as he sat atop a stack of crates. On the other side of the ship, Walter hung from the rope next to the porthole where he had seen his mother. Inside the ship's hull he could see Frimp and Frump fast asleep. His mother's cage was now covered by a large canvas sheet. Everything seemed quiet. Walter pushed along the row of portholes until he found one open. Pucello watched through a porthole on the opposite side.

Bobby stood hesitantly until a gust of wind shook the boom on the main mast, flapping the folded sail and rattling some of the rigging. He jumped at the sound and found himself cornered in an alcove behind the stairs. He kept his eyes fixed on the ship's deck until he was certain there was no one behind him. As he rose back to a full stand, he noticed an ornate door. He reached out for the large brass handle and slowly turned.

Walter squirmed and wiggled his way through the open port-hole, landing quietly on the deck below. He checked to make sure he had gone unnoticed, then tiptoed on the ends of his ten-tacles over to the large cage. Carefully, he lifted the cover until enough light crept in to reveal his mother.

"Walter!?" His mother's voice wafted from the shadows in the cage.

"Mom!"

A long tentacle reached out to touch him. He had never felt more joy in his entire life.

"Walter..." his mother hushed in a fearful voice.

He was surprised by his mother's tone. Surely she must be happy to see him. "What are you doing here?" she continued, "You have to leave here, quickly!"

"I'm here to save you!" answered Walter, confused.

"SSSHHHHH..." came a warning from an open porthole across the hull. "You're going to wake them up!" whispered Pucello.

Frimp and Frump hadn't moved. The snoring from the two of them was louder than anything in the ship.

"Walter, you must go," Ophelia pleaded again.

"I'm not leaving here without you," Walter replied defiantly.

He moved around the cage to the door with the large lock. It was shut tight, and they weren't going anywhere unless he could open it. Walter looked around the dimly lit hull.

"There, on the skinny one," Pucello whispered. "The keys..."

Walter turned to see what the pelican had discovered. He slid over the wooden planks to get a closer look. Tied carefully with a sash around Frimp's waist was a large, shiny brass ring with several keys. Half of it lay underneath Frimp, with the other half nearly covered by Frump's heavy arm. Walter lifted up on his tentacles and stepped even closer, careful not to make a sound.

On the main deck, the ornate door slowly creaked open. Bobby paused, stuck his head in, then followed with a step. No sounds. He hadn't disturbed anyone as far as he could tell. So he brought his full body through the frame. The room was dimly lit by a small oil lamp on a table. In the back he could see the night sky through a full set of bay windows across the stern. To his right he spied an empty bed in a far corner. The coast was clear. He walked over and turned the knob on the gas lamp, illuminating his surroundings. There was no doubt... he was in the captain's quarters.

The room was tremendous. In front of an enormous bed stood a writing desk and a full captain's table, able to seat at least six men. Bonicelli's stamp was everywhere. The walls were filled with trophies: a large, stuffed Marlin, a giant shark's head, hooks, whale fins, harpoons, and a hundred other items that served as a reminder of his great exploits. The room was a treasure chest of fascinating objects from a life of travel and adventure. The yellowing black-and-white photos were most interesting. People from around the world, nearly all showcasing some extraordinary beast Bonicelli had captured with them, hanging from a rope or hook. It was everything Bobby dreamed of becoming. He could have stayed in this room all night.

But what to take back to Blackbeard's Boys, he wondered? His hands drifted from one item to the next around the room; the sharpened point of a fishhook, the smooth texture of a brass diving helmet, the wooden knobs of an old ship's wheel. What proof could he provide? Then, he saw it, in what was probably the oldest photograph in the room. It was standing on the small table next to the bed. Bobby picked it up and pulled it close to his eyes.

Along a dock stood a powerful ship named *Il Canto delle Sirene*, or *The Siren Song*. Bobby knew of a ship by that name. They called it *Il Canto* for short. It had belonged to Bonicelli's father, Rodrigo Bonicelli, and was the one that had crashed along the shore in the great tragedy. Standing before the ship stood four fishermen. Bobby assumed from the fantastic resemblance to Antonio that the large man on the right was none other than Rodrigo. He knew the other adult as well. He had only seen the face in pictures at his own house, but he recognized it clearly as his grandfather, Jonathan James O'Malley, the ship's first mate. The two boys in front of the fishermen in the photo were no more than Bobby's age. One boy in particular had a face as familiar as his own. It belonged to a young Seamus O'Malley. Bobby couldn't believe his own eyes. His father was standing with three of the town's greatest fishermen: Jonathan James O'Malley, Rodrigo Bonicelli, and a very young Antonio Bonicelli. The young Seamus smiled broadly as he held up a fish nearly the full length of his body. The young Antonio's face was covered with more of a pout as he looked over at the other boy, no doubt jealous that his fish was about one third the size.

Bobby's mind raced. There was a lot his father hadn't told him, but even more important, here was his proof. Bobby had made it onto Bonicelli's ship, and his father had been a fisherman just like his grandfather. He could make his own name with Blackbeard's Boys and clear his father's name at the same time.

Filled with excitement, he stuffed the picture in his sack and turned to leave, slamming smack into the table with the oil lamp. Bobby's hands reached out as far as they could, but it was too late. The lamp's glass shattered on the floor.

Frump sat straight up at the sound of the glass breaking above him. To his great surprise, an octopus stood inches from his nose, tentacles spread over his mate, Frimp. Frump screamed at the top of his lungs, waking Frimp in terror. Frimp joined the screaming at the sight of Walter standing over him. The screaming continued until the two ran out of breath and the room fell silent. Walter was frozen in fear.

"H-h-h-h-e, he's trying to steal the keys..." Frump stuttered out.

Frimp grabbed hold of the ring before Walter could react.

Pucello tried jumping through the portal to help, but his clumsy feet and large belly kept him from successfully navigating the opening. He watched helplessly from outside.

Frimp and Walter's eyes met, both determined to hold onto the keys. Walter yanked hard on the ring, but Frimp refused to let go. The tussle sent them both stumbling toward Ophelia's cage. Frimp reached out to strike Walter, but was scooped up at the ankles by one of Ophelia's huge tentacles.

"Heeeeellllpppppp!" he screamed without letting go of the ring.

Frump grabbed Bonicelli's cat-o-nine-tails off of the wall and rushed over. He raised the grip above his head and sent the ends of the whip sailing through the air. The tails let out a loud CRACK as Ophelia caught them with the end of her tentacle.

"Walter, go now!" Ophelia demanded as she fought over the whip and held Frimp in the air.

Walter fought to hold onto the ring, but his small tentacles weren't strong enough to hold against the fisherman's grip. Ophelia tried to get another tentacle around Frump, but lost the delicate grip she had on the whip.

Frump tumbled back into a set of crates, quickly jumping back, cracking the whip at her again. Ophelia felt the sting of the tails striking her. He struck again. In pain, she released Frimp, dropping him on his head, and pulled her tentacles back into the cage. Ophelia's eyes turned to her son in desperation.

Frimp and Frump now stood united between Walter and Ophelia. They began to walk towards Walter. His rescue had failed. The only option out was the staircase behind him.

Bobby was faring no better in the quarters above the hull. The oil from the lamp had spilled out and set fire to the deck. Bobby grabbed the blanket from the bed and smothered the floor, but the fire quickly spread to the bottom of the curtains along the windows. The flames began to rise and consume the back wall of the quarters. Bobby looked around the room for help, grabbing a small washbowl. He threw the water to no avail, then grabbed a pillow and began pounding it against the curtains. Nothing worked. The fire began to catch the wood on the table.

Bobby thought of Bonicelli. He was sure to be furious. Mario and the crew were sure to rat Bobby out. How would he explain this disaster to his father? It didn't matter now. The flames were taking over. In a panic, Bobby grabbed his sack and ran out.

As he blasted through the door to the outside deck he smacked into a large object in the dark. He tumbled hard against the deck, nearly knocking himself out. His head throbbed as he came to. His arms hurt from the fall.

Across the deck, a fuzzy image moved in the dark. Bobby's first thought was that he had bumped into one of the fishermen, and he was caught red handed on the ship. When his eyes adjusted to the dark, he was stunned to see a small blue octopus staring back at him.

The stare down was interrupted by the sound of Frimp and Frump clearing the top of the ladder from the deck below.

"Here, here, little octopus!" shouted Frimp.

Then he spotted Bobby. "Now wait a minute! Who in the blazes is you?"

Walter jumped up at the sight of the two shipmates.

"Frimp, do you smell something funny?" Frump asked.

"Not now, Frump, I'm talking to the boy!" answered Frimp.

Bobby clasped his sack close to his chest and backed up. Frump looked back to see the fire in the captain's quarters.

"Frimp!" Frump gasped as he grabbed his mate by the shirt.

"I said not now you imbecile!"

Frimp hesitated; he couldn't decide whether to go after Walter or Bobby. Frump tapped on Frimp's shoulder again.

"What, Frump!? What is it?" Frimp shouted as he turned around and saw the fire. His jaw dropped as he let out a squeal.

The fishermen raced to save the ship from burning. Walter dashed over the rail, leaping into the water. Bobby watched the octopus disappear into the dark, then scurried down the ladder leading to the docks. By the time the fisherman returned from putting out the fire, the intruders were gone.

onicelli stomped his big heavy boots back and forth across the wooden planks of the ship. In his entire life he had never been this angry. The air blasting from his nostrils was hot. His eyes were red and bulging from his face. His teeth were nearly cracking from the pressure as he bit down with all of his might. Veins stuck out from his neck and steam rose from his ears. He stopped for a second and stared at the charred remains of his Captain's quarters.

"A child! A child! On my ship!"

"And an octopus," added Frimp.

"They was workin' together," added Frump.

Through the seats of their pants the shipmates dangled from a pair of large fish hooks several feet above the floor.

"I HATE CHILDREN!" Bonicelli muttered through a set of gnarled teeth, and looked back over at them. "You'll pay for this!"

"We did what we could. Honestly, Captain," started Frimp. "They was very tricky, and very cunning. We were all set to capture that octopus for you when the boy set fire to the ship. Had it all planned out, he did."

Bonicelli rubbed the deep wrinkles in his forehead, and pulled at the roots of his thick black hair, "What would a boy be doing with an octopus? On my father's watery grave it makes no sense!"

He stomped out of his quarters and slammed the door, leaving Frimp and Frump hanging from the hooks. Down in the hull he grabbed his whip from the wall and approached the cage. With a swift pull he yanked the cover off, sending Ophelia to the far back corner. Bonicelli stared at her with dark, cold eyes. He was so angry he hadn't noticed the Pelican still peering through the porthole.

"What do you know...?" he questioned as he stared at her.

Ophelia stood ready to defend herself if she had to. Her eyes met his with equally strong determination. Bonicelli's anger began to subside as his wits slowly returned.

"No matter, once I show you off at the festival tomorrow, I will be known as the greatest fisherman that ever lived... and your head will hang from my wall."

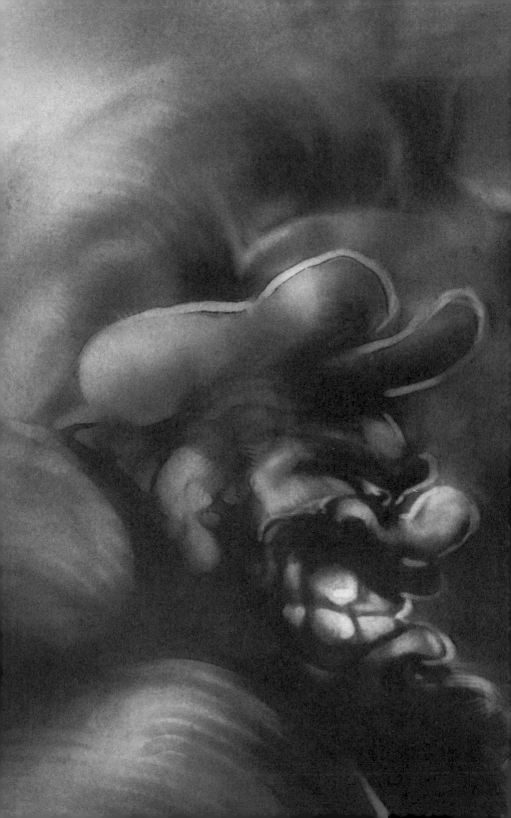

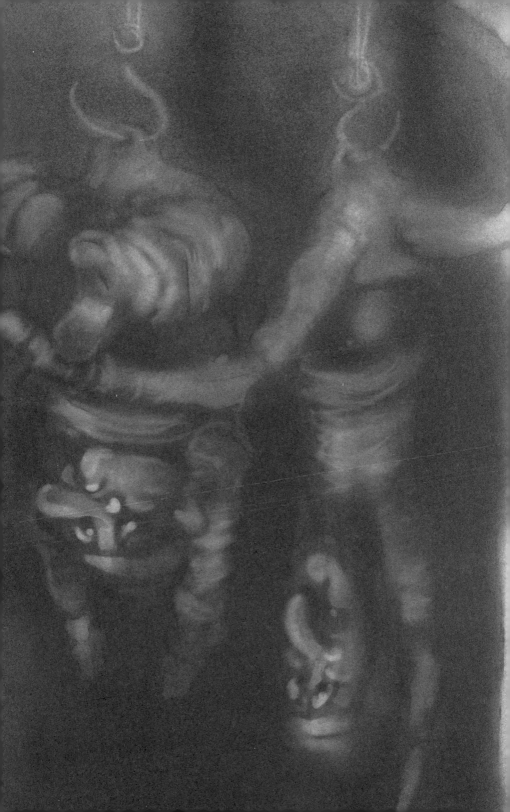

The sun was shining through the curtains in Bobby's window, begging him to wake up. He had turned several times in his bed and even opened his eyes once or twice, but somehow couldn't wake long enough to actually get out of bed. He could almost remember hearing his father's whistle several times that morning, but even that didn't work. He was so tired.

"Hey Bobby," came his father's voice through the hallway, "C'mon son, time to get up, sleepyhead. We need to get down to the square!"

Bobby stretched and rolled over another time, his thoughts drifting to the market square. He loved going down there with his father. There were so many exciting things to see. Bobby especially

loved the candy shop. Mr. O'Malley always let Bobby get something delicious before they headed home. Bobby began drifting off to sleep with thoughts of all the wonderful treats, then suddenly he remembered the night before and snapped straight up, wondering if it was all just a dream. He jumped out of bed and checked his knapsack. The photograph was still there.

Walter woke to seawater lapping against his face. The morning tide had risen in the sandy cave where he had fallen asleep. Slowly, he sat up and looked down at the gentle ripples in despair.

"Helloooo," a call came, echoing off the stone walls. "Waaaaalter!"

Light leaked in from various cracks in the rock and up through the shallow pool at the end of the cave. As it reflected off the water, it danced around the cave in beautiful spirals, giving the cavern a spectacular pale blue glow. Walter had found this place along the jagged coastline in the middle of the night. He stood up, not knowing what to expect.

"Waaaalter...," he heard again.

"Hello?" Walter answered nervously.

Outside, Pucello traversed a dangerous set of rocks leading down from a bluff. Not easy for a short, fat pelican with webbed feet. He followed the narrow path until the light disappeared below.

"Walter?" he called out again.

"Pucello?" came the response.

Pucello was reluctant to take another step. As he leaned over to look down, his foot slipped, sending him tumbling into the dark.

Walter jumped as the ball of feathers came rushing at him. Their bodies slammed into each other and they both let out a scream.

"Walter!"

"Pucello!"

"You scared me," said Walter.

"I scared you?" answered Pucello. "I've been looking for you everywhere!"

"I failed," Walter cried. "I failed my mother. And now she's going to die."

"We still have time." Pucello urged Walter. "There's still a chance. Today is the big festival. Bonicelli is going to be there, and he's bringing your mother!"

The Seaside Festival was the favorite day of the year for almost everyone in town. Everybody dressed in their Sunday best and looked forward to fun and excitement. There were costumes and contests and Mrs. Applebrand's pies. Travelers and playmakers, salesmen and onlookers would all come from far and wide.

Best of all, each year the festival ended with the town council selecting the "Greatest Catch." For months the town's fishermen had all been at sea, trying to capture something magnificent to enter into the contest. The fisherman who hauled in the most fabulous fish or largest whale would be crowned the town's Fisherman of the Year. It was an honor that lasted a lifetime and every Seaside fisherman dreamed of winning.

As Bobby walked the very streets he had been on the night before, he was excited by the buzz of the townsfolk. Jeremiah

Wheeler, owner of the bicycle shop, hopped down the street with a shoe in one hand and pulled on his suspender with the other, in such a hurry he had forgotten to ride his own bicycle. Henny Trottstone, a widow with seven boys, hurried the lot of them toward the market square with their arms full of the scarves she had knitted by hand. Mrs. Picklebare hung her husband's shirts out to dry as Mr. Picklebare loaded barrels of cream onto the back of a cart.

Bobby and his father entered the busy market square and were met with a flurry of sights and sounds. Fish vendors had brought carts with their fresh catches. Mr. Butterburger, the town's short, round butcher, was fighting with his dog over a fresh piece of meat he had just cut for a customer.

"Let go before I feed you to the birds!" he shouted.

A man riding one of Mr. Wheeler's shiny new bicycles whizzed by with a cat on his head. A tall snake-oil salesman wearing bright red tails and a tall red hat barked from the front of his carriage at everyone who passed by...

"*Potions that heal, the magic is real. Cures for the head, the hair, the body, and the skin! Good for the heart, the lungs, the stomach and the liver. A spoonful a day and you'll never be fitter. Specials for today only, it's going fast. Don't be sorry, get it while it lasts. You, young lady, you, young man, not feeling too well, we can help you, we can!"*

There were furniture vendors and clothing carts and fantastic new inventions for the kitchen and the house. Bobby could smell something wonderful floating from the bakeshop but wasn't quite sure what it was... cinnamon buns, perhaps. The town's quartet played a lively shanty from a small stage in the center of the square. A few townsfolk had already started to dance.

"Dad?" Bobby said as he tapped his father's forearm.

"Okay," said Mr. O'Malley, knowing exactly what Bobby wanted. "But don't go anywhere else."

Bobby shot off toward the candy shop.

Pucello typically loved the festival as much as any of the people in Seaside. There would be food everywhere, and because everyone was in such a good mood they were always happy to throw some to him. But today's journey had taken on a darker tone. He knew he had to do something to help Walter and his mother, but what could a pelican do? He stood in front of the fish market searching for an answer.

Bonicelli headed up from the docks like a bandleader heading a small parade. He was dressed in the same clothes he had worn to Ms. Peach's house the night before, drawing a great amount of attention from the townspeople. On his face he wore a grand smile of satisfaction, confident that he was about to be recognized by everyone as Seaside's greatest fisherman ever. Behind him, Frimp and Frump struggled as they pushed the giant, covered cage up the cobblestone street. As they passed, Pucello noticed an opportunity approaching.

Mrs. Habersham was known as the finest quilter in all of Seaside. The festival was her biggest day. Everyone was always excited to see what beautiful new creations she had come up with. Behind Bonicelli's large cage, Mr. Habersham was slowly pushing the Habersham cart stacked to the sky with quilts of all colors. Pucello waddled as fast as he could to get Walter from where he was hiding under the docks.

The candy shop was a glorious place for Bobby. The shelves were lined with huge, clear glass jars filled with mouth-watering, tongue-pleasing delights: black and cherry licorice, gumdrops, jelly beans and gumballs, chocolates and taffies, hard candies and giant suckers. The hardest part was picking which one he would take home. If he was lucky, his father might let him choose two. He usually came here first because he needed time to figure it all out. Barely a row into the store, he turned and bumped face first into Mario.

"Watcha doing, Gracie?" Mario wisecracked as usual. Pete and two boys behind him laughed as if it were the first time they'd heard the joke.

"Mario," Bobby said with a sly smile. He was surprised to hear his own excitement at seeing his tormentor. He was dying to show them what he had accomplished. "I did it."

"Did what?" Mario answered.

"I did it. I passed the second challenge."

Mario's demeanor turned serious, quickly. "What are you

talking about, O'Malley?"

Bobby whispered so that only the boys could hear, "I have something from Bonicelli's ship. It's here, in my knapsack."

"You're a liar."

"It's true," pleaded Bobby. "I went last night."

"You went on Bonicelli's ship... alone?" Mario questioned in disbelief.

"Yes."

Mario looked back at the other boys not knowing what to make of Bobby's claim. "Show it to us," he demanded.

Bobby looked around the candy shop. It was filled with people form Seaside. He remembered the fire on the ship and thought of the trouble he would be in if anyone found out.

"Not here," he whispered again.

"Fine," said Mario. "After the judges announce the winner of the festival, meet us down at the cave. And this better not be a trick!"

Before Bobby could reply, a commotion broke out in the square. Everyone began rushing toward the windows to see the excitement that was occurring outside. Bobby followed the crowd out of the candy shop.

"Ladies and gentlemen!" shouted a booming voice coming from the center of the square. "May I have your attention, please!"

The boys all darted through the crowd, looking for positions from which they could see. Bobby moved along the perimeter of the square, his attention divided between locating the cause of the commotion and finding his father. He found Mr. O'Malley just in front of the general store, greeting Ms. Peach.

"Good morning," they said to each other with a particular stare.

Bobby had seen them look this way at each other before. Their eyes seemed to glow and their cheeks blushed around welcoming smiles. He knew it meant something. Bobby had always been very fond of Ms. Peach. He guessed his father was too.

Bobby's eyes were drawn back to the square at the sound of Bonicelli's booming voice. He jumped up on a barrel and wrapped his arms around a post. From there he could see Bonicelli, standing on a large crate in the middle of the square.

"Yours truly," Bonicelli shouted, "Captain Antonio Bonicelli, the greatest fisherman of all time..." His chest bulged with pride as he spread his arms for effect, "am about to unveil to you, for the very first time in the history of Seaside... the most dangerous... the most deadly... the most ferocious beast in all of the high seas!"

The crowd began to whisper in anticipation. Mothers gathered their children close. Shopkeepers walked outside and left their shops unattended.

Standing on either side of Bonicelli were the town's other great fishermen with their festival entries. Captain Bastille stood next to four hundred pounds of great white shark hanging upside down. Captain Mandrake had captured an electric eel that was at least 30 feet long. Captain Speer was entering a squid that was bigger than most of the people in Seaside. Whatever Bonicelli was entering, it had to be spectacular if it was going to stand up to the rest.

"As all of you will remember," Bonicelli continued in dramatic fashion, "the great tragedy that befell our little town some years ago... that terrible day in which I lost my own father, as well as kin folk to many of you good people. Now, I have spent my days wandering the sea in search of the abomination that rose up and took so much from us..."

Over by the Habersham cart, the butcher's dog had begun

to sniff among the quilts. He cocked his head in wonder as the quilts seemed to move all by themselves, then let out a slow, long growl. Pucello was perched on the end of the cart and noticed the attention the dog was drawing to them.

"Shhh, stop it! Go away. Stop, you stupid mutt!"

He attempted to shoo the dog away, but the dog's excitement only heightened when he saw a tentacle slip from underneath a quilt. He began to bark ferociously at the cart.

"And now," Bonicelli continued from his perch, "I am proud and humbled to say..."

The dog's barking was now loud enough to interrupt Bonicelli.

"I am proud and humbled... WILL SOMBODY SHUT THAT DOG UP?"

The people closest to the cart ran the dog off with a wave of their arms and some stern commands. The butcher himself whacked the dog gently with a broom, but the dog wasn't gone for long, and returned as soon as everyone's attention was turned back to Bonicelli.

"I am proud and humbled to say that after all these years, I, Antonio Bonicelli, have captured the terrible beast of Seaside."

The crowd was now transfixed. Pucello struggled to prevent the dog from any further investigation, but it bit down on the corner of a quilt and began to pull...

"LADIES AND GENTLEMEN!" Boncelli's voice rose, "I GIVE YOU, THE DEVIOUS, THE DIABOLICAL, THE DEADLY, GIANT OCTOPUS!"

Bonicelli ripped off the cover from the cage exposing Ophelia. The townspeople drew in deep gasps at the sight. To heighten the effect, Frimp and Frump poked sticks through the back of the cage, causing her to rise and defend herself. The entire crowd jumped back three feet. Bobby's eyes opened wide.

As Ophelia held the crowd in wonder, the butcher's dog was more determined than ever to unveil the mystery under the quilt. He pulled with his teeth. Pucello flapped his wings and attempted to push him away with his feet.

Before Walter knew what was happening, the quilt covering him slipped off, leaving him exposed. He grabbed the end of the quilt quickly and pulled back. The dog clenched his jaws tight and scratched his paws against the cobblestones. The quilt slipped from Walter's tentacles sending the butcher's dog tumbling backwards. A woman standing next to the cart let out a blood-curdling scream. The whole town turned to see the young octopus. He was nowhere near the size of Ophelia, but his presence outside of the cage ignited a powder keg of fear.

Bonicelli was still enraptured with pride when the panic broke out. He looked up to see chaos as the people of Seaside ran in all directions. The shopkeepers closed their doors and mothers picked up their babies. Carts were left standing in their place.

"Wait!" Bonicelli cried out. "Where are you going? You're perfectly safe! Wait!" he continued. "What about the contest? We haven't finished the judging! We haven't..."

His pleas fell to the cobblestones, unheard. The square was empty with the exception of the fishermen and their entries.

Bonicelli stood in despair. The cage next to him held his grandest capture ever, but the greatest moment of his life had escaped before him.

The next day the town council held an emergency meeting. It had taken a long time for Seaside to forget its great tragedy years before. The fishermen had gradually returned to the sea, the fish market had re-opened, and life had eventually returned to normal. Now, after yesterday's sighting, the fear had returned, and the people looked to the council for protection.

"They've come back for us!" shouted one of the townspeople.

"They've never come on shore before. We're not even safe in town!" shouted another.

"Bonicelli's responsible," complained a third. "He's brought this upon us!"

No attempts to calm them down worked. In less than an hour the council had voted to bring back the sharp-pointed piers

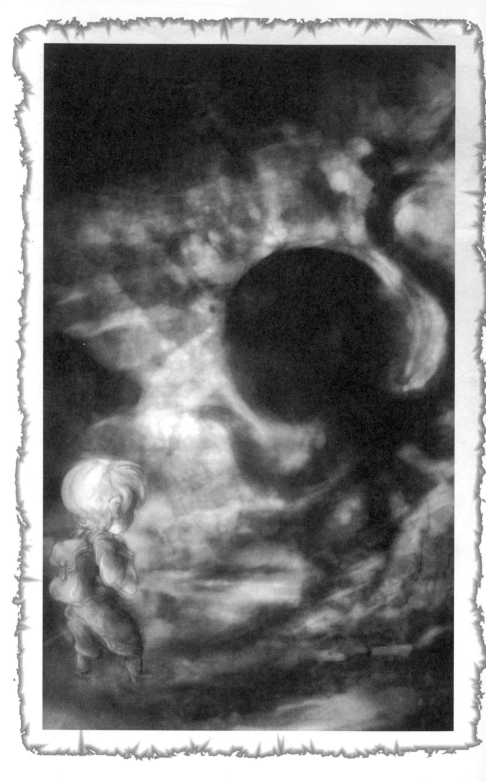

rising from the water at the harbor's entrance. Harpoon guns long ago abandoned would line the cliffs along the shore. Sharp wire fences would be placed along the docks so that nothing could come in or out. The town would become a fortress, guarded against the sea. While a few calmer heads argued against such drastic measures, the votes in favor far outweighed them.

While his father attended the council meeting, Bobby went in search of Mario and the boys at the cave where Blackbeard's Boys met in secret. He had never been there himself, but knew where it was located. As he made his way down the shoreline, the rocks became jagged and more dangerous. The water splashed higher with each wave, spraying a mist over the slippery slopes and salt water into his eyes. The cliffs grew taller with each step. Finally, he came to a narrow opening that looked like a long hallway. It was far away from the town and well hidden among the rocks.

The entrance was dimly lit. Waves crashed with a thundering echo off the cavern walls. Bobby wondered if this was a bad idea, to go alone. If he fell and got hurt it could take days for anyone to find him. Still, he thought the risk was worth the reward. If he wanted to be one of Blackbeard's Boys he would have to move forward. From the blackness a tiny flicker of light glimmered in the distance. Bobby continued on, remaining calm until a strong wind blew through the passage, howling like a wolf in the night.

The terrifying noise sent him running through the dark passage toward the light in front of him. A few steps in his foot slipped, and Bobby went tumbling down the rest of the path. It happened so fast he wasn't sure if he had fallen down five steps or fifteen. He sat up and found himself staring at a large cavern wall and a shallow pool that glowed from light beneath. He looked down to see scrapes and cuts on his knees and elbows. It hurt, but he was okay. His clothes were wet. The shoes on his feet were soaked in the shallow water of the pool.

Bobby moved his body closer to the water, and began to wash the blood from his scrapes. The saltwater stung slightly. As the blood washed away, the cuts didn't look all that bad. Removing the knapsack, he checked to make sure the photo was intact. He was relieved to find it one piece. As he stared at the image, something caught his attention. On the cavern wall across the pool a large shadow flickered from behind him. Bobby jumped to his feet and spun around. In the dark something moved away from him. Water splashed as Bobby took several steps back into the pool.

Bonicelli did not attend the council meeting. He knew exactly how the town would react. In truth, he didn't care. He could only think of how he'd been robbed of his glory. Frimp and Frump were back on their hooks. Bonicelli was even angrier than before.

"But Captain, I thought after the festival you was gonna ask Missus Peach to marry you and we were going to sail off for the Orient," said Frimp.

"Not before I have my revenge," mumbled Bonicelli. "Forty years. Nearly forty years I waited... and searched... the darkest storms and the blackest seas. All for what? To be ruined by a little octopus!?"

"What about the boy?" asked Frump.

"What boy?" fumed Bonicelli.

"The one who burned your quarters, maybe he knows where to find the octopus," answered Frimp.

And then it clicked.

"The boy!" thought Bonicelli, as if the inspiration came on its own. "A boy who plays with octopuses... If we want to find the octopus... we find the boy!"

"Please don't hurt me!" Walter cried from the corner of the cave, shivering in fear. He had stayed as quiet as possible when the small two-legger had tumbled in, but now he was cut off from his only way out.

"You can talk?" asked a stunned Bobby.

"Yes... I talk all the time," Walter answered. The young octopus seemed almost as confused by the question as Bobby was in hearing an octopus speak. The two kept their distance, not knowing what to make of each other.

"Was that you, in the market square yesterday?" asked Bobby.

"Yes," answered Walter slowly.

"Were you the octopus... on the ship, too?" Bobby added.

"Yes," answered Walter again.

"Are they coming for us?"

"Who?" asked Walter.

"The octopuses," answered Bobby. "Are they going to attack Seaside?"

For a brief moment all the tension left Walter's face. He saw the seriousness in Bobby's expression and realized that the question was in earnest. He began to chuckle.

"Why are you laughing?" asked Bobby.

Walter bit back his smile. The thought of the two-leggers being afraid of the octopuses was funny to him. "I wasn't," he responded.

"What were you doing in the square?" Bobby inquired.

"My mother... She was the one in the large trap."

Bobby could see the sadness fall over Walter's expression.

"That huge octopus, the one in the cage with Bonicelli? That's your mother?"

Walter nodded. "She was caught in one of the nets. It was my fault." His voice cracked.

A million thoughts ran through Bobby's head at lightning speed. That beast in the cage yesterday seemed so horrible, so frightening. How could it possibly be something's mother? This little octopus' mother? He thought of his own mother and how much he missed her.

The encounter was interrupted by sounds bouncing off the cavern walls, voices coming from the passage to the cave. As Bobby looked toward the entrance, Walter shot past him into the water and disappeared.

"Alright, let's see it, O'Malley!"

Bobby turned to see Mario and five other boys.

"C'mon, let's see it."

Bobby reached inside the knapsack and slowly pulled out the picture frame. Mario snapped it out of his hands, and the boys surrounded him for a look.

"What is this?" Mario questioned.

"It's a picture of *Il Canto*, the ship that was destroyed on the reef."

"I can read, O'Malley. Why are you giving me a picture?"

"It's from the *Black Fin*. I took it from Bonicelli's bedroom," Bobby replied. "That fisherman on the left, that's Rodrigo

Bonicelli. And the boy in front is Antonio Bonicelli. The one on the right is my grandfather Jonathan James O'Malley who went down with the ship. The boy standing in front of him is my father."

The boys studied the picture for a second.

"How do I know you didn't just take this from your house?" Mario doubted.

"Because I didn't. There are no pictures like that in my house. My father doesn't talk about my grandfather, or fishing," answered Bobby.

Mario was getting frustrated. Bobby was turning out to be craftier than he had planned. Deep down he couldn't believe that the little runt had shown the guts to sneak onto Bonicelli's ship alone.

"Let's go boys," he abruptly spit out as he turned to leave.

"Wait, where are you going with my picture?"

"It ain't your picture now, is it? I'm keeping this until we can prove that you ain't lying," replied Mario.

"What about the third challenge?" shouted Bobby as the boys exited the cave.

Mario didn't bother responding. As much as Bobby wanted

to follow, there was something much bigger on his mind. He turned back to the pool of water behind him. The pool was empty and still, with the exception of gentle ripples touching the sand. The small octopus was gone.

obby woke in a fierce sweat. He had been tossing and turning for hours, replaying his swim to Dead Bone Island over and over again in his dreams. Each time his legs and arms grew tired, and each time he sank under the waves, but just before he drowned something would save him, and he always woke up before the dream could finish. By the time morning came he was exhausted, but couldn't wait to get moving.

As he got dressed, his mind was filled with the events of the last few days. He had completed two of his three challenges, well on his way to becoming one of Blackbeard's Boys and destined to become one of Seaside's great captains. He had seen the inside of both the lighthouse and Bonicelli's ship, and had learned secrets his father had never revealed. Above and beyond, most exciting of all was the octopus. Bobby was pretty sure that none of the boys had ever been that close to one, and absolutely certain that no one had ever spoken to one, not in any of the tales he had ever heard.

Bobby bounced down the stairs and headed for the kitchen. No time for a real breakfast. He grabbed the bread, spread some strawberry jam, and made a sandwich. For a moment he thought about making an extra one, but had no idea what an octopus ate. He wrapped his lunch in a dishtowel, threw it in his knapsack and headed out.

Mr. O'Malley was sitting in the living room putting his shoes on as Bobby ran by.

"Whoa, whoa, son! Where are you headed to?"

Bobby stopped with the door open. "Gotta run, Dad."

"Run where, kiddo? Did you forget you have school today?" his father asked.

Mario was taking his usual route to the schoolhouse with his crew in tow when Frimp and Frump came from opposite sides of an alley and stepped in front of him.

"Hello son," said Frimp.

Mario swallowed a gulp of fear. He knew this couldn't be good.

"Need you to take a walk with us," added the first mate.

Mario looked at his crew. None of them wanted anything to do with it.

"Go on, now!" Frump yelled at the rest of the boys. "This doesn't concern you."

They all scattered, leaving Mario there alone.

"C'mon now," continued Frimp, "No time to waste. Someone's waiting for you."

Eleanor, a tall nine year old in a flowery dress, stood at the front of the class reading from her favorite book when Ms. Peach approached Bobby. He had been unable to focus all morning and did not even notice her presence. He was too busy drawing talking octopuses on paper.

"Is everything alright, Bobby?" she asked.

"Huh?" Bobby responded, almost startled. He carefully moved the drawings under his book.

"Is everything okay this morning? I noticed you're having a hard time concentrating."

"Oh, I'm okay," he answered.

"Well then, let's try and pay better attention to the classroom, shall we?"

"Yes, ma'am," Bobby replied, shifting his body to face the front. He spoke again as she began to walk away.

"Ms. Peach."

"Yes?"

"Do you think it's okay to want to be a fisherman?" he asked her.

Ms. Peach understood why this might be a question in Bobby's mind. He was the son of a fisherman who had turned his back on the sea. Even with the great tragedy, it was a point of ridicule in a town like Seaside. Bobby had carried the stigma his entire life.

"If that's what you want, Bobby, I don't think it's a bad thing," she answered.

"I mean, do you think that the fish we catch, and the other

sea animals... do you think they have mothers and fathers the way we do?"

"I guess I never thought of it that way," Ms. Peach replied. "Why do you ask?"

"No reason," Bobby mumbled as his eyes shifted to the floor.

"What are you, crazy?"

Pucello and Walter had spent the morning arguing in the cave. The pelican was doing his best to talk some sense into the young octopus.

"Do you have any idea what is going on out there?" he pleaded. "There are villagers everywhere looking for you. They have big sharp thingies and ropes and nets. It's too dangerous!"

"If we don't do anything, she is going to die," Walter tried to sound reasonable and confident, but he felt neither.

"And if you go out there, you could die!" rebutted Pucello. The point was obvious but he made it anyway.

"He's our only chance, Pucello. He knows how to get on the ship," said Walter.

"What makes you think you can trust one of the two-leggers? How do you know he won't just turn you over to the fisherman?" asked the pelican.

"What else can we do? Like you said, we'll never make it to the ship without getting caught. We need help. And he's probably the only one who would help us."

Pucello wasn't convinced. He had seen their cruelty too many times. But hadn't he also witnessed some humans being good and kind? Throwing him scraps of food? Maybe Walter was right. If they didn't do something fast, it would be too late for Ophelia.

"Fine," he finally gave in, "we'll find the boy."

"I didn't do it!" Mario cried.

Bonicelli stared out the windows of his charred quarters.

"It wasn't me," Mario continued. "I didn't take the picture." You could hear the sound of his knees knocking together.

Bonicelli turned around, curiously. "Picture?"

"The picture of you... with your father," answered Mario.

Bonicelli's eyes shot over to the stand by his bed. In the excitement of the last two days he hadn't noticed the picture missing.

"What do you know about my picture?"

"It was O'Malley. He's the one who snuck onto your ship. He's the one who took the picture."

"O'Malley?" Bonicelli asked.

"Bobby O'Malley," Mario replied, nodding.

"The O'Malley boy, on my ship?"

Bonicelli seemed genuinely surprised.

"Wouldn't have thought he had it in him... Mario, do you know why I asked you to come here today?"

"I thought it was about the picture."

"The picture?" Bonicelli replied, letting out a forced chuckle. "Oh, that's nothing we can't deal with. I had something far more important in mind."

Bonicelli put his arm around Mario and walked him about the large cabin.

"Have I ever mentioned that I like to think of you as the son I never had?"

"No," answered a nervous Mario.

"Well, not having a child of my own, I've often thought about who would take over the *Black Fin* when I'm too old to journey on, certainly not any of the idiots in my crew. I need someone smart, someone brave, someone cunning. I need a man my ancestors would be proud to call one of their own. The captain of Blackbeard's Boys could stake a legitimate claim."

Mario's chest began to fill with pride, "I've always wanted to sail the *Black Fin*, sir."

"Sail her?" asked Bonicelli. "Why who better to be her captain?"

Mario's feet nearly floated off the floor. Bonicelli continued to lay the bait.

"Boy your age should be ready to go to sea by now. I wasn't much younger than you when I began to sail with my father."

"You mean it?" Mario asked. "You really mean it?"

"Well, of course we would have to convince your parents... and..."

Bonicelli let his words hang in the air to set the hook.

"And?" followed Mario.

"Well," said Bonicelli as he began to test the line, "every captain needs a sailor he can trust."

"You can trust me, sir!" promised Mario. "Anything, I swear."

Certain he had snagged his fish, Bonicelli began to slowly reel him in.

"Tell me, Mario, what do you know about the O'Malley boy and the octopus?"

Walter and Pucello began their search over by the docks. Walter did his best to stay in the water and out of sight. He swam in and out of the piers and around the ships as he followed the pelican above. Pucello searched up and down, climbing crates and barrels, looking through portholes and on ship decks. No sign of the boy. With no luck at the docks or up in the fish market, they decided to move on.

Getting Walter to any other part of Seaside would be much more difficult. If anyone saw him, they would be in grave trouble. Pucello had an idea.

"Wait here," he instructed Walter.

Pucello returned a short while later carrying a large coat in his thick bill and a fishing hat with a large brim. Both were made for keeping out the heavy rains. Not the perfect disguise for Walter, but it just might work. Doing their best to look normal, they concealed Walter in the hat and coat and headed off for the town square.

Together they searched every corner of the market. Bobby wasn't by the fountain, or the cart with fresh flowers. He wasn't by the dressmaker's or the cobbler's shop. He wasn't in the butcher shop or the general store. They stared into the candy shop window for an extra-long time. That's where Pucello's stomach got the best of them.

"Let's go inside," he whispered to Walter.

"What? Why? I don't see Bobby in there," answered Walter.

"We can't be sure from out here," said Pucello.

"I can see the whole store," said Walter.

"Let's double check, just to make sure," Pucello answered, this time walking in without waiting for Walter's agreement.

"What? Wait! Wait!" whispered Walter as his disguise nearly fell off.

But Pucello wasn't waiting. He could smell all the delicious treats, and had to get inside.

Walter had never been in a candy shop before. The wonderful

scents were intoxicating. Sugar blew through the air in so many varieties it was hard to stay focused. Within seconds they had all but forgotten the mission they were on, and wandered through the store sniffing at the glorious confections. They were both mesmerized. In a moment of weakness, Walter slipped one of his tentacles out of the coat to grab a piece of chocolate from an open jar. Unfortunately, a little girl saw the tentacle and began to scream at the top of her lungs.

Walter and Pucello bolted from the store into an alley behind the square. As they turned the corner, they ran smack into the butcher's dog, his huge white teeth shining in their direction.

"Nice doggy, dog," Pucello whispered to the growling mutt, but the dog came rushing at them. Pucello jumped as high as he could and began flapping his wings, leaving Walter alone to face the dog. Walter ran into the first open doorway he could find, leaving the hat and coat behind in the alley.

The shop belonged to the town baker. His wife was in the back preparing pastries while the baker tended to customers at the front of the store. Any hope that Walter was safe was quickly dashed when the dog came flying in through the door. Walter shot into the kitchen.

As the dog came after him, Walter scrambled onto a shelf of pans and pots, knocking several off along the way up. The dog jumped up, barking loudly, his paws banging on the shelf with each attempt to catch the octopus. The baker's wife came into the kitchen to see what the noise was, just in time to see the tall shelf come crashing down. Pots and pans landed everywhere, making an awful racket. On the way down the shelf knocked over a table where the baker's wife had started to prepare pastries. A giant bowl of flour popped up in the air, spraying a cloud of white powder over the entire room.

The baker's wife screamed and grabbed a broom.

"Oh, you horrible animal!" she shouted as she chased the dog out of the front of the store, swinging the broom wildly. "Get out! Get out!"

Immediately she rushed back into the kitchen. Walter quickly slid beneath a pair of ovens and hid out of site. The bakers had a cat named Precious, and the baker's wife was terrified that the dog had hurt the cat.

"Precious! Oh, my precious, where are you?" she cried out in a panic. With great speed she picked up the shelf and moved it out of the way. "Where are you my baby?" she called out. "Did that rotten dog hurt you?"

The cat, who was resting on the top of an ice box, didn't answer. It watched without concern as the Baker's wife crawled around the floor on her knees. Frightened for her pet she searched underneath the pots and pans and along the shelves. Finally she came to the space between the two ovens where she saw something move.

"Precious?" Is that you my love? Please come out, baby. Come to Mommy."

Flour was everywhere in the kitchen, and she naturally assumed that her cat was simply covered in white. It wasn't until she reached in and her hand touched one of Walter's long tentacles that she knew something was off. She looked straight ahead to find Walter's eyes looking back at her. Walter's eyes were blue. Her cat's eyes were green. Walter's skin was sleek and bumpy; her cat's was furry and soft. Whatever she was touching, it wasn't Precious.

The baker's wife screamed at the top of her lungs and flung herself across the room. Walter slid out from between the two ovens and ran for his life through the back door into the alley.

"Monster! A monster!" the baker's wife cried as she entered a square filled with people.

The girl from the candy shop had created quite a stir. More townspeople came out from their shops and gathered in the square to see what was going on.

"It was white!" the baker's wife proclaimed, "with ten arms! It stared right at me!"

"Another sea monster!" shouted one of the townspeople.

"We must find Bonicelli!" shouted another. "He'll know what to do!"

"Bonicelli!" the townspeople cried.

By the time word reached the schoolhouse, the children had been let out for the day. Bobby had spent the entire day planning to search the cave for his new friend, and took off running. As he ran past the market square he noticed the large crowd and stopped. He walked slowly down an alley toward the square and listened.

"Enough," Bonicelli shouted at the crowd surrounding him. "I am a very busy man. I don't have time for this nonsense. The only octopus in Seaside is the one I have in the cage on my ship! It was likely a dog or a large rat. Please go back to your homes and shops. I swear to you if there were an octopus in Seaside, I would take care of it."

As Bonicelli pushed apart the crowd, Bobby spotted Frimp and Frump moving along next to him. Bobby crept backwards out of the square, then turned and started to sprint. As he rounded the corner out of the alley, he stumbled over an odd cobblestone sticking up from the rest. His knees scraped hard against the stones and his wrists shot through with pain as they hit the ground. Voices approached from behind. Bobby reached out his hand and grabbed his knapsack, then hopped on one leg until he was clear of the street and down another alley. He threw his body behind a small fence and placed has back against the wall of a house, pulling his legs up to his chest so that no part of his body was visible to the street.

Bobby sat quietly, trying not to make a sound as the bodies passed by. When he could no longer hear their footsteps he let out a long, hard breath. He placed his hands on top of the small fence and slowly pulled himself up to get a better look.

"Pssssstttt..."

Bobby crouched back down and looked behind him. No one was there.

"Pssssstt…" he heard again.

He stood back up to look over the fence, but saw nothing. He looked left and right and all around, but could not locate the sound's origin.

"Pssstttt…" it came again.

Bobby followed his ears across the alley until he came upon the next house. He touched the wall, then pressed his ear against it, waiting for the sound to come again.

"Hey," the wall spoke.

Bobby backed away from it in surprise.

"Down here…"

Bobby kneeled on the ground. In the crawlspace underneath the house sat a pelican. Bobby looked behind him again.

"Over here," the pelican spoke.

Bobby shook his head and wondered if he'd smacked it on the cobblestones when he fell. Was his imagination getting the best of him?

"We need your help," said the pelican.

As the pelican moved to one side, Bobby saw the octopus

behind him. It was shaking and scared, and for some reason, covered in white. Bobby realized the danger they were in.

"Don't move," he whispered, and turned to look for a way out.

17

"Hello?" Bobby voiced as he opened the door to his house. "Dad?"

Bobby quietly motioned the pelican and the small octopus toward the stairs as he looked around. There was no sign of his father, so he quickly ushered them up the stairs and into his bedroom. Neither Walter nor Pucello had ever been in a two-legger's home before. They took in their surroundings with great interest. Bobby was equally curious. He had never had an octopus in his room, or a pelican.

"Are you all right?" asked Bobby.

Walter nodded.

"Fine," Pucello responded as if there had been no trouble.

"What's your name?" asked Bobby.

"I'm Walter, and this is Pucello," responded the octopus.

"My name is Bobby. So, how come you can talk?"

"What do you mean?" Pucello asked. He and Walter looked at each other.

"Well, how come I've never heard of a pelican or an octopus talking before?"

"Have you ever tried talking to a pelican? Pucello asked.

"I guess not," Bobby answered.

"Have you ever tried talking to an octopus?" Pucello added.

"No," Bobby responded again.

"Then how would you know?"

Pucello's answer seemed almost... logical.

"What were you doing out there?" Bobby asked. "You know they're looking for you."

"We were looking for you," Walter replied.

"Me? Why?"

"We need your help," answered the pelican.

"Me?" asked Bobby. "What can I do?"

"You know how to get on the ship."

"I've only done it once," answered Bobby. "And I almost got caught."

Walter knew what he was asking wouldn't be easy.

"What were you doing on the ship that night?" he asked Bobby.

"It was a challenge," Bobby replied, not wanting to reveal more. "Just something I had to do."

"Is that also the reason why you were swimming alone?" Walter inquired.

The question caught Bobby by surprise. How did the octopus know? As he looked at Walter, something began to flash in his mind. It was the dream that had been keeping him up at night, but this time he could see the end. He had wondered over and over again what happened after he blacked out. How had he gotten to the island? His dream had always left the question unanswered. Now it came back to him. Something had been there. Something had pulled him from the water and set him on the rocks at Dead Bone Island.

"You were there?" Bobby asked, knowing the answer.

Walter smiled in acknowledgement.

"You pulled me from the water."

"I thought you were in trouble," said Walter, happy he was finally able to tell somebody about his rescue.

Bobby began to feel guilt and gratitude at the same time. He was grateful that the octopus had saved his life, but was he supposed to risk his life in return?

"Bobby?" His father called from the hallway. "You home?"

"Quick, hide!" Bobby whispered, as he motioned his two new friends to duck for cover. Walter jumped into an open toy chest and fought to close the lid. Pucello panicked and found nothing but the covers on Bobby's bed.

Bobby ran towards the door and shoved his body against it.

"I'm here, Dad! Coming!" he answered as he squirmed out.

"C'mon son, let's get washed up for supper." They heard as Bobby shut the door.

Dinner was a meat pie that Mr. O'Malley loved to make for his son. It was a welcome relief from the regular servings of fish. Bobby sat in front of his father with a full plate, but couldn't remember sitting down or being served. His mind was consumed with the guests he was hiding upstairs and the swim to

Dead Bone Island. His father had asked him a question at least twice which he had not yet heard or answered.

"Bobby, are you listening?" he heard his father say again.

"Yes, sir," Bobby answered.

"So, what do you think about this whole octopus thing?" Mr. O'Malley asked.

Bobby shrugged his shoulders. "I don't know."

"No need to be worried," his father reassured him.

"I know."

"I spoke to Ms. Peach today. She told me about your conversation," Mr. O'Malley added. "Is there anything you want to talk about?"

"No," Bobby mumbled as he began to play with his food.

"Are you sure?"

"Yes," Bobby answered without looking up.

"Son, do you understand why I don't want you hanging out with Blackbeard's Boys?"

"Because of Grandpa..."

"Well, partly, and partly because I don't like a lot of what Mario and the boys are up to. When we were a crew it was all about becoming fishermen; not getting into trouble. We spent most of our time on the ships, with our fathers."

"How am I supposed to do that," Bobby shot back, "if you won't get on a ship?"

Mr. O'Malley paused for a second, understanding his son's frustration.

"Do you want to be a fisherman, Bobby?" he asked.

"I don't know..." Bobby didn't want to hurt his father's feelings with the wrong answer.

"It's all right, you know," his father added. "We do come from a long line of fishermen."

Bobby's heart began to thump in his chest. His father had never opened up this way.

"Was Grandpa really a great fisherman?" he asked.

"One of the best," Mr. O'Malley said with a pride Bobby had never seen before.

"And you were really one of Blackbeard's Boys?"

"I was the captain."

"You? I thought Bonicelli was the captain," Bobby questioned with surprise.

"Well, he was, after I quit. It's one of the reasons that Antonio and I never speak. His father Rodrigo was the first captain, and he chose me to be the second. Antonio never forgave him, or me."

It was the first time Bobby had looked at his father with a sense of pride in a very long while. As the son of the only man in Seaside who was afraid of the sea, he had been walking around with his head down in shame for too long.

"Then..." Bobby asked with trepidation. "Why did you quit?"

"Wasn't for me, son. After your grandfather died, I never looked at the sea the same way again."

"Are you really afraid of the water?"

"No, not really," Mr. O'Malley answered. "Just too many memories. I'm sorry, Bobby. I know how difficult this has been for you. Seaside was made of great fishermen. I just never wanted you to feel as though you had to become one. When your mother died, she made me promise that I would let you choose, but not before you understood the dangers of the sea. When you are old enough, you will have to decide for yourself what you want to be."

A knock on the front door interrupted their conversation. Bobby watched as his father opened the door to see the baker and two other men from the town.

"Seamus, can we speak with you for a moment?"

His father stepped outside and closed the door behind him. Bobby left the table and pressed his ear against it so he could hear the conversation. The men were forming a search party of some kind, to protect the town at night and be on the watch for any sea monsters. Bobby chuckled to himself. If they only knew what was hiding in his bedroom. This was also bad news, he thought, for his new friends.

His eavesdropping was interrupted by a tapping on the glass behind him. Bobby turned around to see the face of Mario outside the rear kitchen door. He walked over and looked out. Mario signaled Bobby to come outside. Bobby looked back at the front to make sure his father had not stepped back inside.

"Here's the deal, O'Malley," Mario commanded once Bobby was outside. Mario was alone with Pete. "Bonicelli's making me a mate on the *Black Fin*. I get to choose who I take with me on the next voyage. You still think you're ready to be one of my crew?"

"Yes!" Bobby answered, again surprised at how fast the answer came, without even a thought.

"Good. Then you'll be ready for the last challenge."

"What is it?" Bobby asked.

"Rumor has it you know something about the octopus that's been walkin' around Seaside."

"Where did you hear that?" gasped Bobby, not sure what Mario knew about Walter.

"I hear things," Mario answered. "So, you and I are gonna make a deal. You're going to find that octopus and bring him to me, and I'll let you join the crew. You do that and you're in."

Bobby listened without responding.

"And if you don't," added Mario, "I'll tell Bonicelli that you're the one who snuck onto his ship and burned his quarters down."

Mario turned and walked away, without giving Bobby a chance to answer. He was confident Bobby would do exactly as he commanded. Either way, Mario would win. He would get the credit for finding the octopus and earn his spot on the *Black Fin,* or Bobby would go down for refusing to help.

When Bobby returned to his room that evening he found Walter and Pucello asleep in his bed. It was an odd sight, but nothing had been usual about this day. They must have been tired from the afternoon chase. He wondered if the warm quilt and soft sheets were more comfortable than the kelp beds and coral sponge that Walter might sleep on under the sea.

Choosing not to wake them, he moved his toy chest to block the doorway in case his father decided to come up, then sat on the windowsill. In the distance, the moon was casting a reflection on the calm sea that looked like a silver river winding its way into the horizon.

Bobby felt the world begin to press down on his shoulders and his thoughts turned to his own mother. He closed his eyes to remember the smell of her skin, and the way she ran her fingers through his hair. He remembered the sweet lullabies she would sing and how he could feel the vibrations when he rested his head against her chest. He looked back over the bed at Walter, and pictured Walter's poor mother trapped in the cage. Bobby had spent his entire life wanting to be a fisherman. Now he wasn't sure what to do.

ark days returned to Seaside as it became a town impris-
oned by fear. School was cancelled and shops closed their
doors. The streets were empty with the exception of men
patrolling. Experienced fishermen stood high on the rocks,
harpoons ready. Rain fell relentlessly, bouncing hard off the
roofs and cobblestones.

Walter and Pucello had hidden successfully in the house
for the entire night, but Walter was getting sick without the
sea. His beautiful fluorescent blue was fading into an ashy grey.
His smooth skin was dry and flaky. His energy was fading fast.
Bobby knew they were running out of time, and was about to
make the biggest gamble of his life.

"You two stay here. I've got to do something. I'll be right back."

Ms. Peach opened her door to find Mr. O'Malley standing in his trench coat.

"Come in, Seamus. Please, take off that coat. Let me dry you off before you get sick," she said as she brought him in and began to fuss over him.

"Thank you, Clara. I was out on patrol. Just thought I'd stop by and... make sure you're okay," Mr. O'Malley stuttered as Ms. Peach went to get a towel.

"I'm glad you did," she responded as she wrapped a small towel around his head and shoulders. "A little frightening, everything that's going on in town."

"Would you like to come stay at my house?" Mr. O'Malley asked. The words were out of his mouth before he realized what he'd said.

"I'm sorry?" Ms. Peach asked in surprise.

Mr. O'Malley began to stumble over his words again. "I mean... It might be safer... than you being here alone... You being here alone makes me uncomfortable."

"I'm not sure that would be proper," Ms. Peach replied nervously.

Mr. O'Malley stood silent for a moment in front of her, then drew in a large breath as if to gain confidence from the air surrounding him. "Clara," he spoke as he reached out a shaky hand to touch hers, "there is something I've been meaning to ask you for some time. It's been a couple of years now since my wife passed, and longer since you lost your husband. I've long felt as though maybe you were as fond of me as I am of you... Well, if it's not improper of me to ask, I thought, maybe... you would consider becoming my wife."

Ms. Peach's eyes began to tear as she looked at Mr. O'Malley.

"Seamus..." was all she could get from her trembling lips as she wrapped her arms around him in a tight squeeze.

Mr. O'Malley relished in the warm, loving embrace as long as he could, then pulled her back so he could see her face.

"Then you'll marry me?" he asked.

Ms. Peach nodded, wiping tears from her eyes. Then, for the first time in all the years they had known each other, she leaned forward and gave him a kiss.

Outside the house in the pouring rain stood Bonicelli, a

freshly stolen set of flowers in his lowered hand. As he watched the exchange between Mr. O'Malley and Ms. Peach through the front window, he felt a rage fill him as never before.

Bobby watched for his father as he dashed down the wet streets. He had promised that he would not leave the house, and knew what kind of trouble he would be in if he were caught. He turned the corner into a muddy alley and came to a yellow house. Searching across the ground he sorted out a stone just the right size. Looking up into the rain, he threw the rock at a second story window. He waited until he saw Mario peer out.

In a moment, Mario appeared at the rear door of his home. He opened it without stepping out.

"Boy, you really are nuts, O'Malley," Mario chuckled. "What are you doing out here?"

"I found the octopus," Bobby answered.

"What?! Where?" Mario asked as he stepped out from the cover of his doorway into the rain without a coat.

"Doesn't matter. I'll bring him to you."

"I'll meet you at the cave!" Mario jumped.

"No," responded Bobby. "I'll bring him to Bonicelli's ship. I want him to know that I helped you capture him, so he picks me to go with you."

"Fine, Bonicelli's ship," answered Mario. "Meet me in one hour. And O'Malley, you'd better be there."

Mr. O'Malley left Ms. Peach's house with wings on his feet. He hadn't felt this much joy in years. He could hardly wait to get home and share the news. He wasn't sure what Bobby's reaction would be, but hoped his son would understand and be as happy as he was. As the door closed behind him he adjusted his hat and stepped out into the rain. He made the few steps down the street and turned up an alley toward his house. Under the brim of the hat, he saw a large pair of boots step in front of him. Before he could lift his eyes, he felt a huge THUMP on his head, and the lights went out.

"'mon!" Bobby shouted as he hurried Walter and Pucello. "We haven't got much time."

"I don't understand," protested Pucello, "Why are we going to the ship?"

"You have to trust me. I don't have time to explain everything now. It's our only chance."

Walter was wrapped in one of Bobby's coats and a wide brim hat. He was struggling to keep up in the shoes Bobby had borrowed from his father. They had been placed on four of Walter's tentacles as a cushion on the hard stones, but were almost as much of a hindrance as a help. Fortunately for the trio, the town was still locked down and there were few folks out in the streets. Only once was the journey slowed to make sure the coast was clear.

Bonicelli's ship was silent as they boarded. Mario stood alone at the front mast. He stared at the three bodies in front of him.

"So where's the octopus?" he asked Bobby.

Walter and Pucello looked at each other and stepped back nervously, unsure of Mario's intentions.

Bobby looked over at Walter, drawing Mario's eyes to him. Pucello knew something was wrong.

"Walter!" he shouted, but the warning came too late.

Before either could move a net was thrown over them. They struggled with all of their might to no avail. Frimp and Frump appeared out of nowhere and tightened the net around them. Their fight waned as they realized there was no escape. A large pair of boots slowly thumped the deck in front of them.

"Excellent job, O'Malley," appeared the booming voice of Bonicelli. "Toss them in the brig with the others," he ordered Frimp and Frump.

As the first and second mate dragged the net toward the hold, Walter looked back at Bobby in disbelief. What about the plan? Had they just been betrayed? He watched as Bonicelli placed his arm around the small boy and let a bellowing laugh through his broad smile. Bobby turned his eyes away as the net with Walter and Pucello disappeared below.

"I must say O'Malley, I'm quite surprised by your ambition," Bonicelli admitted to Bobby as he walked the boys along the deck. "The two of you are going to make excellent shipmates."

Below deck, Frimp and Frump dragged the net into a cage and locked the door. Once the cage was closed they dropped the ropes just enough for Walter and Pucello to find their way out of the net.

"I knew we couldn't trust him," declared Pucello.

Walter's heart hung heavy in his chest. Any hope of saving his mother was nearly gone.

"Let me out of here," yelled someone from the back of the hull.

Frimp and Frump turned and walked over to their only human prisoner. Mr. O'Malley hung from one of Bonicelli's large hooks, his hands and feet tied.

"Why don't you just keep your trap shut?" said Frimp, "or we might just have to get your boy down here to take care of you."

"Bobby? He's here?" asked Mr. O'Malley, stunned. "Why?"

"Brought us that little octopus there, he did," answered Frump.

"Gonna make a right fine fisherman, that one," added Frimp, "unlike his father!"

As Frimp and Frump laughed, Mr. O'Malley called out for his son.

"BOBBY!!"

Frimp put his hand over O'Malley's mouth as fast as he could, "Now, now, there's no need for that." Frump gathered a long cloth and held O'Malley as Frimp wrapped it around his mouth. "Let's keep it that way, shall we? Or we'll get the cat tails on you."

Walter's eyes turned the corner to see his mother's cage. She had been out of the water for days and was very sick. Her color had turned a pale purple, and she slouched in the corner.

"Mommy..." he whispered.

Ophelia heard her son's voice and opened her eyes. Her worst fears had come true.

"Oh, Walter," she whispered back as she reached through the cage. Their tentacles reached just far enough to touch. "Why didn't you listen to me?"

F rimp and Frump returned to the main deck to find Mario and Bobby standing on either side of Bonicelli at the ship's helm.

"Anchor's away," they heard him shout. "We're casting off!"

Frimp and Frump looked around at the empty deck.

"But sir, you've given the crew leave," shouted Frimp.

"We've got two fine sailors here," Bonicelli responded.

"But, sir, the storm," pleaded Frimp as he looked beyond the harbor. The heavy clouds were nearly touching the water and the swells of the sea were beginning to rack the boat against the piers.

"Then I suggest you batten down the hatches," answered Bonicelli, undeterred.

"But, sir," tried Frimp one more time.

"Looking for a keelhauling, Mr. Frimp?" threatened Bonicelli.

"Anchor's away," the mates responded without another word.

Bobby eyed Frimp as he stowed the keys to the brig on his belt and began to move. The two mates quickly cast off the lines and pushed the ship from the docks. Mario and Bobby did what they could, not having much experience at sea. Within minutes the sails were hauled and full.

"She's free and ready Cap'n," announced Frimp.

"Free and ready!" mimicked Mario.

"Full and by!" shouted Bonicelli.

"Full and by!" shouted Bobby trying to fit in.

"On what heading?" Frimp asked.

"True, and outward bound!" the captain commanded as the ship headed into the wind and began to sail out of the harbor.

"Aye, Aye Cap'n, is the correct reply," Frimp instructed the young boys.

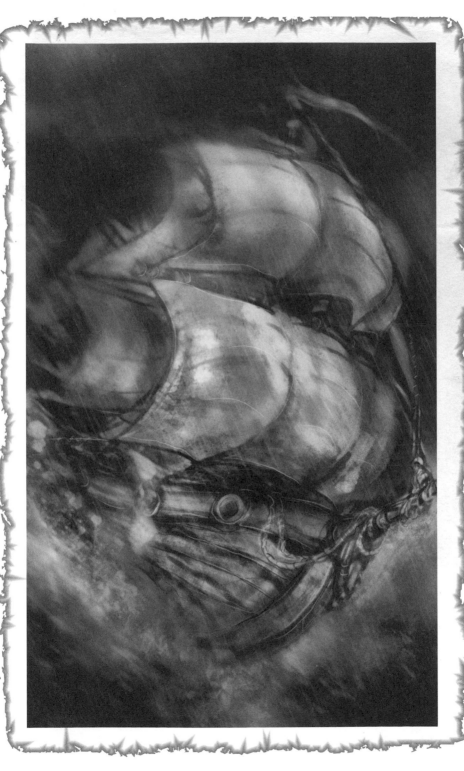

Standing on the cliffs, manning a harpoon, one of the town's fishermen noticed the *Black Fin* setting sail. He wiped the rain from his eyes to confirm the sight.

"Bonicelli is leaving!" he shouted as he waved his arms at the next man down the cliffs. "Bonicelli is leaving!"

"What?" answered the second man.

"Bonicelli is sailing away!" the first man shouted even louder.

The second man turned to see Bonicelli's ship sailing out of the harbor.

Leaving his post he ran down the cliffs and into town. As he made his way through the streets he summoned the town to come see. "Bonicelli's leaving us! Bonicelli is sailing away! He's leaving us!"

The townspeople began to leave the protection of their homes and gather in the streets. As word quickly spread, the mob headed for the docks and shoreline to see for themselves. Within minutes the town bell rang from the clock tower, drawing even more into the streets.

On Dead Bone Island, Higgins was sitting quietly in the lighthouse, listening to the storm as he sat by the fire. With no ships at sea there was no need to worry about the light. The sound of the town's bell took him by surprise.

The old man made his way up the long stairs to the top of the lighthouse as quickly as his crooked, sea-worn legs would take him. As he unlatched one of the window frames, the wind ripped the window open, nearly smashing the glass. Higgins covered his face and grabbed his telescope as he stepped out into the hard rain. The wind nearly took him off the perch. Through his telescope he saw the crowds racing toward the shore and turned to follow what they were looking at. He dropped the telescope to his side as he saw the *Black Fin* sailing past his island.

Bonicelli steered the ship's helm with a confident and joyful grin, the roll of the boat in the growing swells going for the most part unnoticed. Frimp approached his captain carefully.

"If you don't mind me asking Cap'n, where exactly are we heading?"

"To make a fine treasure off the creatures below," Bonicelli answered. "Lots of people out there would consider octopus a right delicacy. Pay us a king's ransom for those two," Bonicelli answered. "And on the way," he added, changing his tone to something much more sinister, "we're going to take care of O'Malley, once and for all."

On the main deck below, Bobby had been repeating the same word in his head, trying to gather up his courage.

"Now," he said to himself again, "Now."

As Frimp slid down the ladder from the helm, he made his move.

"Mr. Frimp, sir. May I ask you a question?"

"What is it, boy?" Frimp asked.

"That line up there, next to the crow's nest," Bobby pointed, "What's it called?"

Frimp looked up in the rain, placing his hands over his eyes to see what Bobby was talking about.

"Which line?"

With shaking hands, Bobby grabbed both the key ring and the sash around Frimp's waist. It was risky, but it worked. With one swift pull the sash unraveled and the keys were free in Bobby's hand. Frimp looked down in surprise as his pants dropped.

"Hey! What the..." he said as Bobby dashed off to the ladder leading below.

Bobby slid down the ladder and jumbled the keys in his hand. He had no way of knowing which ones would open the cages as he rushed toward them. The rattling keys drew attention from all the prisoners below.

"Bobby?" shouted Walter.

"Traitor!" shouted Pucello.

"MMMM!!" his father called under a covered mouth.

Bobby turned to see Mr. O'Malley hanging from the hook. "Dad?"

Frimp and Frump slid down the ladder behind him. "Give us those keys, boy, or you'll find yourself swimming."

Bobby spotted the cat-o-nine tails hanging from the wall

and snatched it before the sailors could. He snapped it wildly, cracking Frump's hand with the end of the whip. Frimp and Frump stood in front of him without backing down.

"What are you doing with my father?" Bobby demanded.

"Give us the keys, boy!" Frimp repeated, but Bobby stood his ground.

"Calm yourself, Bobby," the deep voice of Bonicelli came as he descended the ladder. "We needed some assurances, that's all."

"Assurances?" asked Bobby.

"We needed to make sure you would bring us the octopus. No harm intended. Now we know we can trust you." Bonicelli stepped closer with his open palm out.

With no captain or crew on deck, the ship was now at the mercy of the storm. The bow had begun to turn away from the head wind and the ship was now taking waves directly to its side. Bobby and the others stumbled as it rolled and listed with each fierce impact.

"C'mon, son," Bonicelli urged. "Give us the keys and no harm will come to you or your father. You have my word."

Bobby looked over at Walter, his eyes sparkling the hint of an actual plan, and threw the keys deep into Ophelia's cage.

Bonicelli's eyes opened wide in horror.

Walter smiled, happy he had not been betrayed.

Bobby began to thrash the cat-o-nine tails furiously to keep Bonicelli and his mates from the cages. Mr. O'Malley began to squirm and twist in an attempt to loosen himself from the ropes. The ship began to toss them all about.

Bonicelli's mates watched helplessly as Ophelia grabbed the keys. Her large tentacles weren't much good for the fine skills needed to hold and turn a key, but she worked intensely with several tentacles at once to open the cage.

The first key didn't work, and Bonicelli stepped toward Ophelia. She rose up and launched two tentacles at him. He jumped back without injury, but it was enough to keep him from getting any closer. He needed his whip if he wanted to get those keys back.

"Get me that boy!" he shouted at Frimp and Frump as the ship tilted nearly on its side. Everyone in the hull flew starboard, slamming into the walls and sides of the cage. Mr. O'Malley's body swung with such fury that the ropes holding his hands ripped along the hook, sending him bouncing along the floor. Bobby was hurt and getting dizzy, but he stood again to defend himself.

Mr. O'Malley worked his hands free from the torn ropes and removed the sash around his mouth, but struggled with the ropes binding his feet. Frimp dove at Bobby, receiving the end of the cracked the whip on his arm. Bonicelli and the two mates closed in around the boy and his father. Bobby raised the whip again and swung it forward. Bonicelli caught the tails in his hand before Bobby could finish the crack. The powerful fisherman gripped the end of the tails and raised Bobby off the ground, letting out a horrible, devious laugh. Bobby wriggled in the air for a moment, then suddenly... let go.

By the time Bonicelli and his mates noticed the large shadow across the floor, it was too late. They turned to see Ophelia towering over them in absolute fury. The barrels cracked into pieces as the bodies flew against them. It was frightening how small and weak Bonicelli looked when locked in one of her large tentacles, and how easily she tossed the fishermen about, even in her frail state. All three had been knocked unconscious when she turned her attention to Walter's cage. In desperation she attempted to rip the cage door from the bolts on the floor, but she had become too weak. Bobby approached the cage from behind Ophelia, startling her. Ophelia rose up in a terrifying pose.

"Mom, no!" shouted Walter.

The ferocious mother paused at the sight of the small boy, noticing the keys in his hand. As she calmed, she allowed him to pass and open the cage.

Ophelia grabbed Walter and held him tightly as he came out. Pucello ran out and threw his wings around Bobby.

"Great plan!" he said to the boy. "I knew it all along."

Without a word, Ophelia dragged Walter up the ladder and pulled the two of them out into the rain. As they fled, Walter looked back at Bobby.

Mr. O'Malley ran to his son and wrapped his arms around the boy and the pelican. He had never been so terrified and proud all at once.

"Help me son," he said to Bobby as he pushed the crates and barrels away from the injured fishermen. Together they dragged all three into the cage that had held Ophelia, and locked the door.

When Mr. O'Malley and Bobby reached the main deck with Pucello, all was not well. Mario sat helplessly on the deck, clinging to one of the masts.

"Help! Please!"

The ship was drifting directly toward the very reef that had created the great tragedy so many years ago. At this speed the hull would be torn to shreds and everyone aboard would likely perish. They only had minutes to react.

"We need to come about!" Mr. O'Malley shouted into the wind.

Ophelia and Walter moved quickly through the rolling current toward the safety of the reef.

"Mom!" Walter cried out as he looked back. "The ship, it's going to crash! They'll all drown."

"No more interfering with two-leggers, Walter. Haven't you learned anything?" Ophelia replied without stopping. Walter pulled his small tentacle from her grip and stopped on a coral bed.

"I'm going back," he stated defiantly to his mother.

"Walter, you'd better listen to me now," she warned.

"He saved us, Mom! He saved us. That boy, Bobby, he risked everything to set you free. Without him I wouldn't have you. I can't let him down now."

"They can't be trusted," Ophelia proclaimed.

"Yes, they can. Maybe not all of them, but some of them are good, like Bobby. You can go if you want, but I can't let him down."

The sails on the ship had lost their wind and were slinging against themselves violently. The ship continued its spinning drift toward the shallow rocks of the reef. From the top of the lighthouse, Higgins had been watching the ship head toward danger without its crew. He was now flashing the big lamp at the *Black Fin* to warn them of imminent disaster. Townsfolk had begun to climb the cliffs next to the harpoons, and were looking on in despair.

"Take the helm!" Mr. O'Malley shouted at Bobby through the wind. "And do exactly as I tell you."

Pucello lost his footing on the wet deck and began to roll with the sway of the ship.

Bobby ran up to the helm and grabbed the smooth, wooden knobs on the giant wheel. The rudder was bouncing wildly underneath the ship and the wheel's spin took Bobby off his feet. He fought hard to gain back control.

Mr. O'Malley began to loosen the sheets and push the yards. Bobby had never seen him do any of this before, and was in awe of his father's skill and confidence under these conditions.

"Mario! Grab that line," Mr. O'Malley shouted, but Mario was frozen in fear, and Mr. O'Malley was forced to continue without help.

"Turn the wheel starboard, Bobby, hard, starboard!" his father shouted across the deck.

"Starboard? Won't that point us right at the reef?"

"You have to trust me, son. There's no time. We need to catch the wind or she won't turn!"

"Somebody, do something!" shouted Pucello as he slammed into a moving crate.

As the ship turned into the reef the wind caught its back. Mr. O'Malley let loose the main sail and as the wheel hit full starboard, it popped open.

"Forward HO!" he shouted as the sail pulled ferociously on the ship. Bobby spun the wheel to the left and stopped it dead center. Mr. O'Malley held firmly onto the ropes, the skin on his hands almost splitting. The ship lunged forward, the mast making a loud cracking sound as if it were going to break. Mr. O'Malley's eyes were locked on the reef. As soon as the ship had the speed it needed he shouted his next command.

"Again, Bobby! Full starboard!"

Bobby spun the wheel right again as hard and fast as he could, sending Pucello rolling across the deck again. The ship seemed to stop in the air as the aft began to come around and the wind left the sail. A huge wave crashed over the starboard side, nearly capsizing the *Black Fin*. Mario shivered in fear as he held on for his life.

"Hold!" Mr. O'Malley shouted through the pouring rain as he began to pull in the sheets, hand over hand, with all of his strength. Bobby watched as his father moved with great speed, ducking and weaving, pulling and hauling as if it were second nature; loosening this rigging, tightening the next while the large boom came flying across the deck. As the ship made its way almost completely around, the sails caught dead wind and began to flutter.

"Let go and haul!" Mr. O'Malley shouted, and Bobby swung the wheel back to its center.

The ship was now facing away from the reef, but the waves were pushing her backwards. If she stayed here they would be shattered into a thousand pieces.

"We're going to die!" Pucello shouted. In desperation he flapped his wings and pushed off the deck, but his feathers were wet and heavy. A gust of wind blew him at the helm, and he bounced off the wheel before landing behind Bobby.

"Pucello, you have to fly!" shouted Bobby. "You'll be safer."

"You try flying in this!" Pucello shouted back.

"Steady!" Mr. O'Malley shouted to his son when the final line was in place. He ran along the port side toward the aft of the ship. Bobby kept the wheel straight but began to look back in fear. It wasn't catching the wind. The waves continued carrying it backwards.

"C'mon!" Bobby shouted at the sails as if to command them.

As Bobby looked forward he saw a huge wave heading toward them and knew they were in trouble. "Dad!" he shouted.

Mr. O'Malley looked forward at the wave and then back toward the water. They were out of time. He could see the shallow rocks rising just feet away from the back of the ship. The next wave would crash them right into the jagged rock bed. His eyes darted up at the sails. The ship had not finished making the turn and they were still struggling to find the wind. As the wave headed straight at them, he ran up to the helm and held Bobby at the wheel. It struck the boat with immense power. The bow shot skyward and the water broke over the beams, rushing along the decks. The ship stopped hard and the wood shuttered from aft to bow, but when the wave passed, they were still whole.

Mr. O'Malley and Bobby looked at each other, confused.

"Look!" shouted Pucello. "Look below."

Bobby and Mr. O'Malley ran to Pucello and looked overboard.

Below the stern stood Ophelia, pushing on all tentacles to keep the ship from smashing. The ship relaxed for a second as the wave receded and prepared for the next.

"Hurry!" shouted Walter from the water. "She won't be able to hold much longer!"

"Dad! The wheel!" Bobby shouted at his father. The ship was now continuing its turn, but the wheel was spinning in the wrong direction. Mr. O'Malley launched himself back at the helm to take control.

The townspeople on the cliffs began to gasp in horror as they saw the large octopus, her arms wrapping the back of the ship. The fishermen at the cliffs began to release their harpoons. One slammed into the ship as Bobby looked down. Another cracked the beam next to Pucello, taking one of his feathers with it. The others missed and landed in the water.

"Stop!" shouted Bobby back at the cliffs, "She's helping us!"

Ophelia continued to hold as another wave approached.

Higgins, who had been watching these events unfold, turned the great lamp toward the cliffs and blinded the harpooners so they could not see where they were shooting. The next wave hit the ship harder than the first. Again water crashed over the bow and flooded the decks. Bobby, Mr. O'Malley and Pucello nearly washed overboard. Ophelia kept the ship from being torn apart once more.

At last, the sails filled with air. The masts groaned as the wind pulled the ship forward. The hull sped down the back of the wave and up the next wave. They were safely off the rocks and under sail. The town started to cheer from the cliffs.

As the ship cleared the reef, Mr. O'Malley wrapped his arms around Bobby and placed his hands on the ship's wheel.

Pucello shook his feathers in the rain and wrapped his wings around their legs. "Oh, thank you, Poseidon."

"A talking pelican?" Mr. O'Malley asked.

"I'll explain it to you later," answered Bobby.

Mr. O'Malley looked down at his son with great pride. He had long ago forgotten how wonderful it was for a father and son to be at sea. He was grateful for this moment, and swore to himself this would not be their last journey.

"Close haul, Captain?" Bobby asked his father.

"Aye, aye, Captain," his father responded.

Together they sailed bravely into the storm.

"It's safe to let go now," Pucello joked at Mario. "Some fisherman!"

Bobby looked back toward the shore one last time. Walter stood alone on a rock jutting from the reef and watched the ship sail safely away with pride. Bobby waved to him with a smile.

easide returned to happier days. Down came the piers blocking the harbor and the harpoons lining the cliffs. The fishermen once again took to the sea and the market square regained its hustle and bustle. Ophelia never came back to Seaside, but Walter often did. He spent many days in the caves along the shore with Bobby and Pucello. Over the years he met many of the town's children. Every once in a while, Walter would venture into the town. When everyone saw him, they would welcome the octopus with open arms. Everyone that is, except for Bonicelli.

Mr. O'Malley married Ms. Peach, and spent the following years teaching Bobby everything he had learned from his father about ships and sailing. Bobby however, never became one of

Seaside's great fishing captains. He used what his father taught him to sail the world and study the seas. He became one of the world's foremost experts on the animals of the ocean, and dedicated his life to helping them. Whenever he visited Seaside he would spend time with Walter. Often in the same old cave, they would laugh about their younger exploits, and Bobby would tell Walter all about his travels. Their friendship lasted throughout all of their days.

No one in Seaside ever forgot the story of the young boy and his octopus.

THE END

ACKNOWLEDGEMENTS

The journey is long and well-traveled. The steps alone are the hardest taken. Thank you to the loved ones in my life who bring smiles to my face, shower me with kisses and carry me when I am tired. It is you who have help me stay the course and continue onward toward my dreams, even when the light is hard to see, and the road is covered in vines.

This book would be half finished without the incredible talents of my dear friend and visual maestro Hannah K. Shuping. I can't tell you the pleasure I feel when you bring my stories to life. Thank you for all of your dedication and hard work.

I have been a storyteller all my life, but one person above all has mentored me in the art of writing those stories down to be read by friends and strangers alike for generations to come. Thank you John Bemis for your incredible friendship and guidance.

To Beth Kallman Werner and Author Connections LLC, not only for your help in preparing this book for its debut on the stage, but for your endless enthusiasm and support. It's just fun to have you on board.

To my team at The Book Designers. Once again, thank you for your amazing work!

To our masked patron. You are a gentleman and a scholar. Thank you for helping us push forward.

For my partner in crime Michael G. Jefferson. You are indispensable on this adventure. All of the dreams we hold in our pockets will be unfolded for the world to see.

Thank you to the entire Barroso Clan, for all the years of support. You will forever be my family.

And of course to Maria, Sam and Joc, without whom none of this matters.

184